HIGH NOON AT MIDNIGHT

I looked at Maximiliano Sacco.

He looked at me.

"Max," I said, "why are you telling me all this?"

"Because, *Señor*," my little scene-stealer replied. "Walter Woody is the legend. He must remain so. To that end, Richard Roland and his women must be dealt with. Therefore..."

Sacco's round, hard, black, steely eyes lasered me.

"We are offering you one million dollars to liquidate Roland and his associates. Jail or not, we cannot take the risk. You see?"

I saw all right.

For the first time in my life, someone wanted to hire me as a Hit Man.

I was being offered a Contract.

Oh, Godfather, where art thou?

IS THIS AN OFFER NOON CANNOT REFUSE?

HIGH NOON
AT MIDNIGHT

Michael Avallone

PaperJacks LTD.

TORONTO   NEW YORK

AN ORIGINAL

PaperJacks

HIGH NOON AT MIDNIGHT

PaperJacks LTD.

330 STEELCASE RD. E., MARKHAM, ONT. L3R 2M1
210 FIFTH AVE., NEW YORK, N.Y. 10010

First edition published October 1988

This is a work of fiction in its entirety. Any resemblance to actual people, places or events is purely coincidental.

10 9 8 7 6 5 4 3 2 1

ISBN 0-7701-0993-4
Printed in the USA

Table of Contents

THE CAST OF CHARACTERS

.... according to their Achilles Heels ....

.... and some of them never get over them.

THE TIME MACHINE

"Death is greater than leaving town . . . ."
— Ed Noon in *Downey's*,
on a hot August night
in 1987.

This, a payment of a debt, to Sabatini, Dumas, Cervantes, Rostand, Wren Dickens and Gary Cooper and *The Plainsman*.
And to all men everywhere who bled for Mankind, without looking back.
And for all readers everywhere who believe in Ed Noon. Especially Stephen Mertz and David Avallone, Noonmen incarnate.

HIGH NOON
AT MIDNIGHT

1.

MEMORY TRAIN
GOING BY

*It was very easy to remember George Long
and what we had been to each other . . . there
I was . . . a combat line sergeant in Uncle
Sam's U.S. Cavalry, the Mechanized 33rd of
the Twentieth Armored Division. . . . we
chased the German Army clear across war-
torn Europe. . . . Hitler and his Third Reich
were on the run and the general feeling all
over Command Headquarters was that the
knockout punch wasn't far off . . . when it did
come, with Adolf committing suicide in that
crowded bunker in besieged Berlin, the third
team of the fourth platoon of B Troop was on
the outskirts of Munich with the Seventh
Army . . . mopping up they called it . . . I had
my armored car, the M-8 with Gehrig painted
on its sides, the machine gun jeep, Gentleman Jim, and the mortar jeep, Gershwin,
to round out the combo, positioned in the*

hills . . . . *Reconnaissance was our fulltime job. . . . George Long was my radio man . . . a temporary assignment because my regular Sparks had caught some shrapnel in the shoulder the day before . . . . Long was good at the job. Very good . . . . what was even better was the way he saved my life that day . . .*

. . . I was stepping down from the turret of the M-8 when a shot rang out . . . German gunfire . . . I know the noise . . . I'll never forget that particular bullet . . . it came very close . . . spanging off the metal armored car . . . inches from my helmeted head . . . but only because Technician Fifth Grade George No-Middle-Initial Long spotted the sniper in the woods before I did. Too late to even shout a warning . . . it had been raining that day too . . . a light, chilling rain. . . .

. . . Long's eye and aim were perfect . . . and he needed only that one shot to get his man . . . and save my New York hide. . . .

. . . his kill was an SS man who should have surrendered days ago . . . a ragged wreck, half-starved . . . a fanatic who probably died yelling "Heil Hitler!" with his arm stiffened in the Nazi salute . . . but I never did check out his corpse in the woods . . . there never was enough time for the niceties of living. . . . not in those hard times. . . .

". . . George," I said when Long snapped the bolt on his carbine, re-slinging the weapon. *"I owe you one. . . ."*

. . . the grimy, serious face before me was blandly calm.

"Sure, Sarge. Pay me later."

His tone was So-What and All-In-A-Day's-Work.

"When this cruel war is over?" I mocked, still a little shaken by the near-miss. I had come close to Graves Registration. Too close . . . .

"Yeah," George Long laughed. "Then . . . ."

. . . but that was in April of 1945 . . . .

. . . Then has become Now . . . . September of 1987 . . . and I am not a soldier anymore . . . .

. . . only but another of the walking wounded . . . .

2.

MAX, MAX

This one started in a way most of them don't.

Over a very dry martini at forty thousand feet above the mighty Rockies. About where Kansas meets Colorado.

The jet was a Jumbo, the cocktail was a Beefeater. A double. And between those superlatives of aircraft passenger flight and high noon drinking, sprung up the entire difference between Life and Death. Maximiliano Sacco's life, my death. Let me tell the story before the men in the white uniforms come to carry me quickly away. In case you'd like to choose up sides.

You have to in these troubled times, I'm afraid. So they'll have some idea where you belong when Accounting Time comes. They have to know where you stand in the scheme of things.

"Mr. Noon?"

"That's me."

"I am Maximiliano Sacco."

"That's nice, Max."

"Please, Mr. Noon — this is important —"

"Sure. Sorry."

"I observed you stepping on the plane at Kennedy. I could not believe my good fortune. *Nuestra Madre* has placed you in my path —"

"Sit down. And slow down. Have a Beefeater. You're going too fast. Sure you haven't mixed me up with somebody else?"

"Never — I will do as you say. I am nervous, as you see. Yes, a drink, perhaps. I would have spoken to you sooner but I had to wait until the little old woman went to the toilet and — I cannot wait until we arrive at Los Angeles International —"

He was talking about the schoolteacher who was ticketed in the seat next to me, on the aisle. I had the window view because I am nuts for cloud banks and limitless blue space without the speck of a stone building in sight. Miss Woodburn, a genuine little old lady from Pasadena was on her way back for the beginning of Fall classes but beyond that had said very little. She had spent the first few hours of the flight with her nose buried in Jong's *Fear Of Flying*, which scandalized me because Miss Woodburn was on the wintry side of sixty. Still, it was when she disappeared down the wide middle passageway to the powder room that Mr. Maximiliano Sacco suddenly materialized before me. My nose was sunk in the Beefeater, brought gaily by the curvy, wholesome, freckled stew named Malvina but *Señor* Sacco's shadow was more than a little awesome. I didn't know a thing about him right then and there but time and circumstances were to take care of that. He edged into Miss Woodburn's seat and fairly disappeared into its roomy environs. He was smaller than the schoolmarm, which wouldn't have seemed possible. But when a man is barely more than five feet tall on old-style Cuban heeled shoes and is dressed in plantation-white ducks and sweeping, wide-brimmed hat to match, the *El Exigente* image is almost a parody. All *Señor* Sacco lacked was the flowing, bristling bandit moustache. But the rest of his face was walnut-hued, unwrinkled and dazzlingly healthy. The flash of his teeth under a hawk nose and eyes blacker than olives, was almost blinding. But not even the glow of well-being could hide the speckle of moisture on his smooth cheeks. Or the nervous flitting of those brilliant eyeballs. Maximiliano Sacco was scared spitless.

Malvina swept down the aisle, winked at me and I held up two fingers, signalling for another round. She nodded and switched off again. She had a rear view like a proud horse. Prancing.

Sacco was in no frame of mind for girl-watching.

So I put him at his ease by making noises

like the detective I was supposed to be. What else could he want a man of my stamp for?

"Why did you shave off your moustache, Max?"

"But how could you know that?"

"You're a Latin. Spanish if I make out your accent. Looking the way you do, a moustache would be ideal, wouldn't it?"

"Yes. I shaved it. Only this last week — but — then you may have heard of me — know who I am and what I am?"

"No way. I'm just making educated guesses. So start telling me things. Your drink will be here in two shakes of Malvina's derriere. Come on, now. Miss Woodburn isn't going to stay cooped up in that john all day. She won't read Jong in there though it's as good a place as any. Particularly, if they're low on toilet paper. I'm sure you don't want anybody else on the plane to know what it is you're going to tell me. Isn't that so, *Señor* Sacco?"

"Es verdad" he breathed, with a mixture of happiness and lingering sorrow. "You are most correct. Very well. To the point I will come. I am in your so fine country on behalf of my government. I am what passes for the ambassador, the diplomat, in this matter I shall explain to you. To that end —" Suddenly, the coal-black eyes opened wider. "But, pardon, how could you have known about my moustache? You have never seen me nor is there any photograph in existence that I know of —"

"Max," I said, as gently as I could. "The skin area under that superb nose is at least three shades lighter than the rest of your face. In short, it has only just seen the sun after many a year under the bush. *Comprendez?* A, B, C logic. Nothing miraculous about it at all. Now, you were saying something about ambassadors and governments —"

"*Magnifico, Señor,*" he crowed. "But how simple —" He peered around us grimly then and tilted back to me. The dark eyes glowed. "What I have to tell you concerns Walter Woody."

"Walter Woody?" I echoed, lower than his own furtive stage whisper.

"*Sí* — we understand each other, I think — and I speak to you at great risk. Both to myself and yourself — you are interested, *Señor* Noon?"

"Yes," I said. "I am interested."

Maximiliano Sacco shuddered briefly, began to open his mouth, but I motioned him to stand fast. Malvina had come bouncing back, all freckles and curves, smiling as if she had invented sunlight. The tiny *Señor* grabbed at his drink as if it were a life preserver, bestowed a glittering smile on Malvina and took an enormous pull on the Beefeater. There was no sign of Miss Woodburn. Still in the john with Jong.

"Understand me, *Señor* Noon," Sacco whispered, trying not to lean into me. "Walter Woody is the why of all things. Why I am on this plane, why I must speak to you,

why before we touch down the wheels in the
city of Los Angeles, I must know if you will
help —"

"Max, please. If you've something to tell
me — tell me. No more preambles and
ahems, huh? Time's a-wasting."

Beyond my shoulder, the gorgeous wide-
open blue sky shimmered. Atmosphere-
jewelry. The diadem of the universe. The
crown of space.

Maximiliano Sacco told me what he had to
say about Walter Woody.

I had to listen.

Walter Woody was ten times the legend
and mystery that Howard Hughes had been.

And was.

3.

ROSEBUD FOR WALTER WOODY

Maximiliano Sacco had a lot to say. In slow and deliberate one-verb-and-adjective-at-a-time English. It's necessary for me to translate for him, speed him up or we'll be here all day. Whatever truth there was in what he had to say, it was an earful. A fourteen-carat declaration of some kind. A Revelation, the Dead Sea Scrolls, the Secret That Would Topple Empires — that is if he was spouting Gospel. And if a couple of UPI or AP wire service boys were around to take it all down. But he only told it to me. As I am telling it to you. Wherever the real gold of it all is, the little brown man in the white tropical suit, handed me the story of the century.

Or the decade, at least.

People have been killed, whole family lines destroyed, for much, much less.

Ask any man who would be king. And I don't mean Stephen.

As Walter Woody had and done.

In any case, here is the story according to Maximiliano Sacco, told on a jumbo jet winging high above the United States on a sunlit afternoon. With God in his so-called heaven and not much right with Life. When nobody had any thought about dying:

WALTER WOODY (owner of corporations, hotels, islands in the Pacific and one-half of a gambling State) has not been seen for thirteen years. He is a legend in his own time, with a billionaire background — Flying Ace in World War Two, maker of movies, lover of hordes of lovely movie stars and princesses and heiresses, and a king-sized reputation as an eccentric; indeed a Charles Foster Kane-William Randolph Hearst-Howard Hughes image all rolled in one.

Indeed, the time is ripe for this profitable 'apple' to be plucked by perhaps the most clever con man of all time.

Taft-Regent, a prestigious name in the publishing field, announces for its Summer list a tremendous as-told-to autobiography, THE WALTER WOODY STORY, which it seems is the work of a free-lance novelist and ex-Washington newspaperman named Richard Roland. Roland has convinced Taft-Regent's editorial staff that he was personally selected by Walter Woody to write an authorized biography. Roland is in possession of miles of taped interviews, minutes and recordings of all of his meetings with the fabulous Woody on a remote island in the South Pacific during the years of '85 and '86. It took Roland a full year to accumulate his material and write his book — for which Taft-Regent advanced him the princely sum of five hundred thousand dollars.

Taft-Regent, assured of one of the biggest publishing scoops in the history of book buying and selling, has authorized affidavits and Walter Woody's 'true' signature on many a document signifying his approval, authorization and happiness with Richard Roland as his biographer. The modern world breathlessly awaits the publication of THE WALTER WOODY STORY, hoping once and for all to learn the True Story of The Legend. In advance of publication, one of America's leading weekly magazines has paid a fortune for the exclusive rights to the installments-publication of Roland's eagerly-awaited book. Redbook, no less.

In this loaded climate of expectancy and interest, the bombshell explodes: Walter Woody's staff of advisors and partners call the Press.

Without emerging from the seclusion which has marked his life, an interview is arranged on the top floor of the Waldorf-Astoria, with the byliners of many a noted local newspaper summoned to listen to a taped statement of Walter Woody declaring that the entire account of Roland and he collaborating on the book is a hoax. Then a phone conversation is piped into the suite so that the newsmen can talk to a voice on the line which sounds like Walter Woody.

Woody is both outraged, perplexed and ready to sue Taft-Regent, Richard Roland and everyone involved for trying to put one over on the public. In effect, he says: "I don't know anyone named Richard Roland, I never met the man, I never planned to write a book and I have no idea what this is all about. I have only come forth for the express purpose of halting this charade before it goes any further.

The next day, all of America is tuned in, via TV, newspapers and gossip, to the thorniest and most incredible story of the decade.

Richard Roland, through his lawyer and publishers, stoutly insists he told the truth, he met Walter Woody in the Pacific and together they both wrote THE WALTER WOODY STORY.

Walter Woody makes no further statements but he and his stockholders sue Taft-Regent for two billion dollars. The District Attorney's office is standing by — watching the suits and counter-suits, ready to take action if it is warranted.

Meanwhile — as the public avidly follows the story day-by-day:

Richard Roland flies out of town in a private plane, with his lovely wife, ex-movie actress, Winifred Gentry, and holes up in seclusion in the wilds of Vermont, away from the press, notoriety and the law. During this time, the investigation rapidly gets underway, with subpoenas issued to all parties involved. Woody's staff and Taft-Regent's battery of claims investigators go to town, trying to substantiate or undercut each other's version.

It is learned that: (as all the facts start adding up) —

Richard Roland deposited his five hundred thousand dollar advance in a Swiss bank and drew on it repeatedly, with a lovely blonde who claimed to be Winifred Gentry making the withdrawals.

Winifred is a brunette — who is the blonde? — and if it was Roland's wife in a wig — why the disguise? What is going on, anyway?

Taft-Regent, using experts, insists the Walter Woody signatures in its files on all the related documents are genuine. Is Woody a liar or what? Or just plain eccentric, with a foolish memory?

A week later, the mysterious blonde, located by Swiss authorities, proves to be a French model, a health spa owner named Viviane Orley, who also claims that she has been Richard Roland's mistress for years and has no knowledge of him ever going to the South Pacific to write a book with Walter Woody. He couldn't have — he was with her most of the last two years, during which time he was estranged from his wife.

Through newspaper articles and a brief interview on the Channel 7 News the public learns a bit more about Richard Roland.

He is thirty-six, darkly handsome, a regular Casanova type who, oddly enough, is the possessor of great writing skills. A book of his — TOWARD SUNSET — won a prize in 1970, and he seemed a promising novelist fit to join the ranks of Roth, Mailer, Capote, etc. But the promise was never fulfilled and he wound up spending his days working on a newspaper in Washington, D.C., a job he was subsequently fired from for making personal advances to his City Editor's charming wife.

To thicken the plot, his wife, Winifred had either starred or been featured in four of the films which Walter Woody made in the early '60's. Mrs. Roland, it seems, is considerably older than her husband. The newspapers make all sorts of speculations about this exceedingly pointed coincidence — could the estranged Winifred Gentry have provided her husband with a lot of the data and material in his purportedly bogus book? (The confession mags went crazy with this angle.)

Again, nobody knows for sure — they won't know until the day in court — when Walter Woody will have to appear to make his accusation and prove that Richard Roland is no more than a genius of a con man.

Meanwhile, Taft-Regent has postponed indefinitely the publication of THE WALTER WOODY STORY. But no book in history ever had more advance interest ....

The whole wide universe is bugged by three simple questions:

Did Walter Woody authorize Richard Roland to write a book?

If he didn't, what is Richard Roland up to?

If he did, why is Walter Woody denying it now?

Nobody, it seemed, could answer those basic riddles.

Nobody except Maximiliano Sacco.

Quoth El Señor:

Walter Woody is dead. He has been dead for a long time; a fact which the people who control his vast empire have wanted to keep from the Public. The image of a 'live' Woody, though unseen, has been used to great advantage by the Empire for years.

Richard Roland knows this, through his wife, who aside from being an old Woody flame, inadvertently learned of his death without the Empire knowing she did. She does not love Roland — but she loves Money.

Thinking the Empire would keep their mouths shut to protect themselves, Roland wrote a 'phony' book, duped Taft-Regent with documents, brilliant forgeries of the Woody signature (thanks to Winifred's possession of old love letters) and walked off with five hundred thousand dollars, convinced he would get away with it.

The Empire, not knowing what secrets such a book might contain, fought back, hoping to make Taft-Regent and Roland back down. When they did not, the Empire was forced to make a move.

This 'move', had been front page news, only two months ago:

A 'double' comes forth, fools the court and the jury, denounces Roland and his wife and everything else, and then walks out of court. The book is banned from publication and the Rolands are warned to keep their mouths shut 'or else'. Richard Roland will get a jail term for pulling a swindle — but he will stay alive, knowing what he knows, but not able to tell anyone else. The price for breathing the air around him.

And that was all that Maximiliano Sacco had to say to me. Up until the clincher, that is. The bombshell.

Incredibly, Miss Woodburn still had not returned from the powder room. The Beef-eaters had gone dry, too. Malvina was busy elsewhere.

I looked at Maximiliano Sacco.

He looked at me.

"Max," I said, "why are you telling me all this?"

"Because, *Señor*," my little scene-stealer replied. "Walter Woody is legend. He must remain so. To that end, Richard Roland and his women must be dealt with. Therefore —"

Sacco's round, hard, black, steely eyes lasered me.

"We are offering you one million dollars to liquidate Roland and his associates. Jail or not, we cannot take the risk. You see?"

I saw, all right.

For the first time in my life, someone wanted to hire me as a Hit Man.

I was being offered a Contract.

Oh, Godfather, where art thou?

4.

FLASHBACK FOLLIES

Before we fly any further on that jumbo jet with Maximiliano Sacco dangling his incredible carrot before me, we have to backtrack here. It's necessary because without it you won't understand anything that follows.

I started westward ho for some fun in the sun and a breather from my private detective universe, carrying a pair of letters in the attaché case that goes where I go when I leave the Crooked City for considerable lengths of time. My one business accessory.

Two specific letters.

One on blue paper in a matching envelope that isn't mine.

The other on plain beige stationery, ditto, that is.

The first letter is an official item, bearing the pompous letterhead which says: MANHATTAN CRIMINAL INVESTIGATION

DEPARTMENT. The outfit on Twenty-Seventh Street has been located on the East Side ever since Diamond Jim Brady cracked his first lobster with *sauce margeret*. MCID has no connection with the N.Y.P.D. but it is supposed to help anyone on the journey to a career in police work.

It goes something like this:

August 12, 1987

Edward A. Noon
160 West 46th Street
New York, N.Y. 10017

Dear Mr. Noon:

I have received your very interesting letter of August 10, 1987. I read it with a great deal of wonder. It puzzles me as to the reasoning behind your unwillingness to allow me the privilege of meeting you. It would be a great injustice not only to me but to students enrolling in a private detective training course to have perhaps an imposter teach them. The only way I might know that the proper and talented Mr. Noon was standing before them is if I had the opportunity of learning who he was beforehand.

After several phone calls and communications of all sorts in reference to you and your position as instructor here, I am sincerely more than anxious to meet with you. There is the possibility as well that you might enjoy meeting me. Your secretary, Miss Mercer, indicated on the phone when I called last week that I had somehow offended you by my 'demands to interview a man who is willing to give his time and expertise to the course' and 'doesn't have to be interviewed for the job like some aspiring actor answering a Broadway cattle call. . . .'

If in any way I have offended you, I sincerely apologize, and on the other hand, for the offense you have extended in my direction, I forgive you. I hope that you can find it within your personal and professional ability to extend me the courtesy and the good fortune of making your acquaintance in person.

After all, even I would like to meet the very famous Mr. Ed Noon.

Sincerely,

(Mrs.) Paula Kluger
Director

PK/JD

The second letter, the plain beige one, was my reply. Without imposing heading and squared initials. Melissa didn't type that one:

19 Aug 87

Dear Mrs. Kluger,

You probably meant your charming communique as a *riposte* but it went over like a lead balloon with me.

Again, I'm baffled by your logic and your hesitancy to render a simple Yes or No. Above all, I shall be eternally confounded as to why you made it such an onerous task to re-apply for the conducting of a class which I have already earned my spurs in, twice over. I was doing the course before Jack got assassinated and rookies came in from left field, demanding to give me a once-over, pass-over test to see if I was right for the job, set the thirty teeth I still have left on edge. Sorry, lady.

So let me do the honors.

I am no longer interested in the Class.

It doesn't matter anymore whose fault it is.

The damage has been done.

Good luck to you.

P.S. Has anyone told you yet today?

I'd fled town before she'd had a chance to come back with one more of her pretentious sallies. No, I hadn't been very graceful but I was weary of a world of unprofessionals. Johnnies-and-Jennies Come-Lately, who didn't know how to hack their jobs. It was finally getting to me, how ill-suited most people were for their life's work. I'd run out of patience. So I ran to the nearest plane.

How did Houseman say it?

"Into my heart an air that kills
From yon far country blows:
What are those blue remembered hills?
What spires, what farms are those?
That is the land of lost content,
I see it shining plain,
The happy highways where I went
And cannot come again . . . .

I didn't have to be a Shropshire lad. I got the message. Maybe Mrs. Paula Kluger never would. Damn her officious ass.

"A million dollars," I said to Maximiliano Sacco. "Is that all?"

"*Señor* —"

"Clam up. Here comes Miss Woodburn."

"But I must have an answer before this plane lands —"

"But I must think, Max. House rules, *amigo.*"

He seemed to see the wisdom in that, smiled thinly and rose. Not even the Cuban heels helped. Miss Woodburn, the little old lady from Pasadena, as slight and slender as she was, towered behind him. Her smile ignited the pathway between the rows of seats. *Fear Of Flying* was tucked beneath one angular elbow, with a page marker jutting. A bit of orange ribbon of some kind. Somehow, I still remember that. Considering all the mammoth, monstrous and incredible horrors which were going to fill that jumbo jet ride to California.

"Hello, again."

"Mr. Sacco's been keeping your seat warm, Miss Woodburn."

"Oh, that's all right. The view is wonderful, isn't it? So clear, so far-off —." Miss Woodburn's voice was pure schoolteacher. The best kind. Warm, clear, brimming with interest and enthusiasm. My tiny Latin Santa Claus bowed, showed his teeth, murmured something fervently courteous and backed off down the aisle. I didn't watch him go. Malvina's glorious rump intervened once again. She was bowing over a little girl, patting pillows, making stewardess noises of comfort and reassurance. Miss Woodburn plopped into her seat and propped Jong on one knee. Her bird-like face beguiled me. She looked so alert.

"I don't suppose you'd want a drink," I suggested.

She shook her head. We were old friends now.

"What a picturesque little gentleman. So Old World."

"Uh-huh." I finished the Beefeater. The easy rumble of the engines, ceaseless, somehow eternal, were lulling me. I felt sleepy despite Maximiliano Sacco's fairy tale at forty thousand feet. There are quacks, nuts and locos and I was trying to think, to sort out all that he had told me and what I could remember about the Man of Mystery, Walter Woody. The Roland character was something else.

"Did you just meet Mr. Sacco, Mr. Noon?"

"What you would call Instant Acquaintance. What else do you make of him? You seem the kind of person who can make rather accurate first impressions of people."

"Well, now —"

"No, no. Go ahead. I'm not pulling your leg. I'd like your conclusions about the little guy." Miss Woodburn beamed. Flattered.

"You know he *is* very interesting. Not just his clothes and that all-white ensemble and those dark features of his — he's just so different than most people — what do I think? You promise not to laugh?"

"Miss Woodburn," I growled, affectionately.

"All right. I think he's terribly frightened. I mean really. As if he thinks the wings might fall off or there was a bomb on board. He has the look of someone waiting for something to happen — I don't know — but there was a child in one of my classes once. A rascal and a devil. He'd put a firecracker in the lower drawer of my desk. With a very long fuse. Set it up and put it there just before I came back to class from a talk with Mr. Rogers in the hallway, our principal back in — well, no matter *when* that was. What I'm trying to say is, Mr. Sacco has that look. I saw it in a flash. Just as he got up from his seat and left us. Poor man. Is he really afraid of flying? Or some such like that?"

"No, I'd say not," I smiled. "So don't lend him Jong. Even if it really doesn't cover the subject. But you're correct, of course. Mr. Sacco has a lot of worry in his motor."

Miss Woodburn's eyes rounded and oohed and aahed.

"Did he tell you what was troubling him?"

"Not in so many words. Did you notice anything about him besides that looking-over-his-shoulder aspect?"

"Well —"

"Go on."

"Two things, Mr. Noon." Miss Woodburn was enjoying herself immensely. She didn't know I was a detective by trade, either. She was simply enjoying that age-old guessing game. Who-and-what-are-my-fellow-travelers? "For one, he has recently shaved-off a moustache. A fairly thick and full one, I should say For another —"

I stared at her. She was impressing the hell out of me, now.

"Don't stop. You're doing fine."

"Didn't you notice? He isn't wearing a single ring or jewelry or trinket of any kind. Somehow, that strikes me as not quite — right. Looking the way he does. An obvious Latin, a man from a culture which conditions its males to wear such things — I mean — wouldn't *you* have expected at least one ring on those swarthy hands? Or a pearl stickpin? Or an earring? I would I mean, I'd expect such an ornament of some kind on a gentleman like that. Wouldn't you have, Mr. Noon?"

"I certainly would," I said slowly. I couldn't have agreed with her more. And I just lost three points on my license. Damn. I've been asleep at the switch. Thank you very much, Miss Woodburn.

"Surely a religious medal or some such. Saint Christopher? Especially when traveling abroad —" Miss Woodburn concluded on a note of personal satisfaction, now that she had heard her own deductions out loud. And then her face crumpled as she stared up at me, rising from my seat. "Oh — where are you going? Did I say something I shouldn't have, Mr. Noon?"

I must have confused her, at that. There might have been something pretty grim about my expression. I can't say for sure. Petite Miss Wooburn registered chagrin. I smiled and patted her knee, still holding my glass with the other hand. Whoever her small charges were in Pasadena, they were thrice-blessed. The lady was a crackerjack brain. On all counts.

"On the contrary, Miss Woodburn. You scored a hundred. And you may have saved me from a terrible social blunder. I owe *Señor* Sacco a great apology. One I intend to make to him right now. The sooner the better. See you later, Miss Dove."

With that, I left her. Clutching her Jong, thoughtfully.

I tried not to run down the long, roomy aisle, poker-facing all the massed S.O.B.'s crowding their over-priced seats, trying to relieve the universal monotony and collective fear of aircraft-in-flight, zooming high, hard and handsome miles above all of God's Little Acres. No longer Wyoming real estate. Now, the upper bridge of Utah, corridoring into Nevada. I knew the route, blind-folded, having flown it many times.

I'd lied to Miss Woodburn, of course.

I hadn't lied to *Señor* Sacco.

He had lied to me.

When a man removes every single article of jewelry, every item of costume ornamentation from about his visible person, there has to be a reason for it. And a far better one than the story he had given me.

Mr. Sacco had something to hide, obviously.

Or, at the very least, he was up to something.

I had to find out what that something was before we jumboed another one hundred miles above the clouds. It was Nervous Time.

Like Paula Kluger's stuffy, unfunny letter, Max had something perking under his wide-brimmed white hat.

Something besides Walter Woody's legend and hiring me to kill a character called Richard Roland who maybe wrote a book.

Something I just had to know.

And fast, fast, fast!

Let the sundial in that ancient Scottish garden, long, long ago take the rap for what I was thinking and feeling. The one that's been scaring people for the last seven centuries.

It is later than you think.

And Orwell had really called the shots forty long years ago.

5.

HELL IS WHERE YOU FIND IT

Maximiliano Sacco was neither in the spacious bar nor the lounge section. Nor did I spot him entering any of the powder rooms. So I waited, stone-lion style, near one of the plexiglass portholes showing miles and miles of blue sky. The little man had been very fast on his Cuban heels. A safe guess was that he had vanished into a convenience.

There was more than one so I decided to catch him exiting. I had never guessed as wrong in my life.

I was still toying with Miss Woodburn's pure Holmesian logic, trying to come up with a proper answer for all of her observations. Being in the clouds mentally as well as physically sort of ruined the eyeball detail.

All around me, conversation drifted upward as passengers talked, smoked, dined, maybe flirted. There were so many S.O.B.'s it was like intermission time at a Broadway play. A Between-The-Acts atmosphere from the word go.

And then the trouble hit.

With the kind of a bang you might take with you to your grave.

A woman screamed suddenly. Just like that.

A ripping, tearing cry of terror, the kind of noise-stopper that makes everybody else in the room shut up as if someone had turned their contact buttons off. I came away from the sky-window with a reflexive push that was absolute instinct.

I saw the whole picture. In an instant flash.

Men and women, a clutch of children, had all fanned out, spreading apart like the Red Sea. And between them, lurching toward me, was the little *Señor* himself. Quick images, flipping.

In that tremendous split-second hush, with only the smooth purr and drone of the Jumbo's jet engines, Maximiliano Sacco saw me, and his cocoa-brown face, now two shades whiter, tried a brave smile. I couldn't see for the life of me what he had to smile about. It was gallows humor in its finest hour. Sacco the Magnificent.

For he stumbled reaching me, his figure doubled and the handle of some kind of knife stood up from the high part of his back like the flag marker on the eighteenth hole.

Sacco had been stabbed —

Memories, mind pictures, roll-backs of cerebral film of all the times and all the places in the past when I had seen this precise bloody moment, came back at me like rebounding tennis balls in a mad nightmare of a game.

Memo Morgan hitting the deck in the lobby of the *Ritz*. Blassingame, the British agent masquerading as a nun at Shea Stadium, Benny my favorite bartender stuffed in the refrigerator of his place on West Fifty-Sixth — all of that came at me in a blinding rush even as I caught the dying Maximiliano Sacco in my arms. As small and light as he was, his heavy fall carried me to my knees. Dying somehow makes people heavier. Don't ask me why.

"*Señor —*" Staccato, spurting gasps parted his well-shaped mouth. " — *they stop at nothing ... you see ...*"

"Max, shut up — get a doctor, some-body —"

From all sides, voices swirled, loud and low, boxing me in. The screaming woman had turned off, too. I heard a child whimper-ing and someone else sobbing.

"*. . . Woody . . . . Woody . . . . liquidate Roland . . . for him . . . for me . . . .* Señor Noon ... ?*"

"Sure, Max. Stop talking, will you?"

The knife had dammed up the flow of blood from the wound but the internal damage of cold steel tearing through a man's vital parts, that was something only a medico and X-rays could solve. I cradled the little man in my arms, snarling out loud for that doctor or someone, anyone, with medical expertise who never did show up. A jet full of S.O.B.'s but luck of the draw, not a single M.D. this flight. And Time wouldn't wait for Maximiliano Sacco.

We all run out of time, in the final analysis.

The pint-sized mystery man suddenly reared up, seizing both my coat lapels with clawing hands. He only let go when his dark eyes rolled, the lids closing over them and a half-choked moan wrenched from his throat. He died without saying another word.

Not so much as a bit of a dying message that Ellery Queen always tantalizes his reading audience with — no such luck.

By that time, it was all over, indeed.

For all of us.

Maximiliano Sacco died first — we were next.

There was a great and thunderous *whooshing* roar and the whole universe pitched at right angles. It was as sudden and momentous as the fall of the executioner's axe, a starting gun in a race, a clang of a dinner bell, an atomic explosion in the wastelands of New Mexico. The world will end with that sound.

A blasting, booming explosion of violent upheaval and destruction skyrocketing at us from somewhere close to the nose of the ship. The thunder and disintegration volumed at all of us from that direction before the whirlwind took over.

Every light in the cabin winked out.

Everyone screamed at the same time. The brave, the terrified, and the hybrids, all. Maximiliano Sacco was swept from my arms like a rag doll activated by wires and strings.

I shot backward with no intention of doing so, arms windmilling for a ski jump that wasn't there. It was a mad rollercoaster ride. Bodies flying, cartwheeling, scattering in all directions. A weird barrel house in a carnival gone haywire.

And then the bottom dropped out of the world.

And we were all going down.

Down, down, down.

In a straight descent. To the real pits.

An aerodynamic impossibility, according to the experts.

Literally power-diving in a jumbo jet for the real estate known as Nevada, far, far below. Or maybe still Utah.

Bomb on board.

It was the last coherent thought I had, as the women and the men and the children kept on screaming into eternity.

The last deduction of a detective.

Before the world ended.

His world, and everybody else's.

6.

THE EVENING NEWS ACCORDING TO MIKE MONKS

It was hard to believe he was dead, much less gone. Guys like him just don't buy the farm. I'd known him for over thirty years and he'd walked away from explosions, machine gun barrages and even once when they dumped him into a river chained up like a Harry Houdini trick. Customers like Ed Noon just don't die. They cannot be killed. Ed had more than nine lives, he'd had dozens of second chances. So even when the headline story broke on the Channel 4 news report and became a Page One story the next day, I still didn't buy it. There had to be a ringer somewhere in the deal. Especially given the crazy circumstances. But there was only one thing I could do about it after I came out of shock and had a good cry. I phoned Melissa Mercer at home. She wasn't at the office. I didn't expect her to be. When the man who is your whole reason for life, for living itself, is dead and gone, what the hell are you supposed to do?

She was in and answered the phone on the second ring. That would be Melissa, all right, expecting him to call from God knows where, saying — guess what, I got out of that plane crash, after all. Mel was the most beautiful black woman I have ever known, both in soul and in the flesh and Ed had fallen in love with her long, long before Guess-Who's-Coming-To-Dinner liberalism.

"Mel, it's me," I said, as gently as I could. "Mike Monks."

"Oh, Mike," she whimpered in a voice as dead as Nixon's reputation. I could tell she had been crying for a long time.

"Honey, I don't know what to say."

"Oh, Mike," she said again.

"I know, I know."

"It's so hard to believe — him — Ed — the horseshoe man — I keep expecting —"

"Me, too. No matter what the reports are. It's weird, okay, as weird as they make them —"

"That pilot — " I heard her controlling herself. "Setting that jet down like that in all that desert. Without losing a single passenger. Except —"

"Don't talk about it, Mel. Unless you want to."

"But I do. I do. That little man — Sacco — and the bomb — he's gone and Ed's gone — the only two people lost when it could have been everybody on that jumbo — weird? It's like some Black Magic trick. I keep expecting Ed to pop up with some wild story — and all he was trying was for some vacation time in Sunny Cal. Like what he said the day he left . . . ."

"Mel," I got a little tough with her, knowing I had to. I could hear hysteria beginning to build in her voice. "It's no good thinking about it or talking like that. You'll only make it harder on yourself. You don't have to tell me about him or how you feel. You know what I thought of him. What I still think of him. God's finest man on this rotten earth. But that won't help anything, now. I want to help *you*, now. Understand?

"Yes, Mike." It was a low moan from a graveyard.

"Is there anything I can do for you? Anything —? You want company — I could stay with you overnight . . . ."

There was a low chuckle from the other end of the wire. The old Melissa, almost. The Diahann Carroll clone, like Ed called her.

"Why, Captain — you want to spend the night with me?"

"Yes," I growled. "I don't want you coming apart at the damn seams. Or going up the wall. You need some company — you have to stop thinking about him. And don't look for miracles. Mel . . . ." I softened up then.

"Yes, Mike?"

"That plane came down from forty thousand feet with a third of the nose gone where someone planted that bomb. Ed was on the spot, according to eyewitness reports — Sacco had been knifed — it's the damnedest piece of flying that made that pilot manage to pancake that big jet into the desert without getting anybody else killed — but they couldn't find Sacco and they couldn't find Ed — Mel, do you hear what I'm trying to say?"

"I think so."

"Then say it out loud. I want to make sure you understand me."

I heard her deep breath.

"Yes, I heard you. I understand. You're telling me that Ed and the little man had to be blown out of that hole into the sky. When nobody else was. You're telling me that Ed is riding on a cloud or telling his bum jokes in heaven, if there is a heaven. Okay? You're saying all that but I'm telling you I won't believe he's dead until I see his body, until I can touch him and he doesn't move — heaven can wait, as far as I'm concerned —"

"Mel —" It hurt like hell now. To hear her talk like that. She had always impressed me as being a very level-headed woman, but what did I know about Love and Faith and Hope? I'd never tried the first one and being a cop for over forty years had soured me like hell on the last two. "You're only hurting yourself more."

"No. It's my way. I'll play it that way. And I'll stay here by this phone. He'll call. You wait — he'll call — I just know he will. Ed can't be dead."

"Mel, I'm coming over."

"No you're not." There was steel in her now. "You're a sweetheart for making the offer but I have to have my cry alone, Mike. You understand?"

"Yes — no — hell, I *don't* know. Mel, you're sure?"

"I'm sure. Goodbye, Mike. And thanks."

She hung up and all I could do was stare at the phone in my hand. She made sense and she didn't make sense. She was being foolish and she was being smart. She was just being Melissa, I guess.

Whatever she was being, she was also being a woman.

And I have never been able to handle them. Not at all.

Not the way Ed could.

Ed Noon. *Jesus, was he really dead this time?*

Damn him. Melissa was right about one thing, though.

It was still pretty incredible, plenty tough to believe that after a hundred tight squeezes he was dead.

Dead and gone.

He had been one helluva private detective.

7.

MAD MAX AND CRAZY EDDIE

Again, I looked at Maximiliano Sacco. Again, he looked at me. Behind us, the monolithic buttes of Utah reminded me of all those great John Ford westerns, with or without John Wayne. They were towering, sun-scorched and majestic. And just a little bit terrifying. Mother Nature in the raw always is.

"*Señor*," quavered the little brown man who was now several shades lighter. "It is a wonder we are still alive."

"Yes, Max. A wonder, a miracle and a how come?"

"We should be dead . . . exploded into so many little pieces . . . *Dios!*"

"Yes, Max. *Dios*, indeed."

"Do you not marvel at what has happened? As I told you on the plane — the enemies of *Señor* Walter Woody stop at nothing — as you saw, a bomb, *Señor*! With a cargo on board of hundreds of people: women, children . . . ."

"Shut up, Max," I barked him down. "And let me think. Our goose is hanging pretty high as it is."

It had been a harrowing last hour of life.

Sixty minutes of complete terror, monumental confusion and gnawing uncertainty. To detail it was to live it over again but it had to be done; it had to be reasoned away before it grew into a bug-eyed monster which would devour us both. Me and the little man from Latin America. The white-suited employer of assassins.

There are miracles. There have to be. How else to explain that nameless jumbo jet pilot who brought that big ship down onto some vast stretch of desert which might or might not be the great alkali plains of Utah in the Salt Lake territory? A mammoth aircraft with a huge chunk of its nose blown away. A heart-stopping, bump-bump-bumping of a pancake landing with passengers bouncing around like loose tennis balls. I lost my head in the uproar. As soon as the ship came to a jarring dead-stop, with the S.O.B.'s screaming and yelling in pain and fear, I grabbed Sacco by the hand. Sacco, who had suddenly muddled into view looking dazed, powder-burned and horrified. I grabbed him and pushed him out of an open emergency door. I hadn't looked back, wanting to put as much distance as possible between us and the plane. I can't really say what I was thinking just then, if I was thinking at all. My mind was full of hired killers, terrorists and further attempts on the little man's life. It never occurred to me that he might have planted the bomb — but that wouldn't have made any sense, would it? He had wanted to hire me just to prevent such a thing from happening — but *something was wrong, wasn't right.*

Amidst the commotion and panic of the emergency set-up, with passengers milling about, tumbling out of that big ship and nobody paying much attention to anyone else, I literally dragged the little guy some hundreds of yards from the crash site and didn't stop to rest until I had deposited us both behind a hillock of salt earth. From there, I started to breathe again, lungs aching for air. He did too. We could hear the commotion from the crash scene as far away as we were. It didn't sound like any clambake.

Rescue for them all would be a matter of time if the ship had been able to radio its location in as I was sure it had. The pilot had had plenty of time if his communications set-up hadn't been damaged by the explosion. I didn't know how far we were from civilization. I only recognized Utah. It had to be Utah, considering all those buttes and the course we had been on from New York.

"*Señor*, why do we not remain with the plane?"

"Do you want to die, Max?"

"No. Of course not. But you are saying —"

"Maybe your bomber is on board — maybe it's a Kamikaze deal. I don't know — anyhow, let me think."

"*Kamo*? But what is that, *Señor*?"

"An old Japanese custom about dying. Suicidal but effective. Now shut up," I said. "My brain is going around and around —"

And not much later, when the first air rescue helicopters came in, I was still trying to make some sense out of everything. But I couldn't. I had nothing to go on. But the choices were obvious even to me. We couldn't stay in the desert, we couldn't hike to the nearest town — I didn't know what or where that was — but we did the next best thing. We pulled ourselves together, marched back to the giant Jumbo squatting on the desert like a grounded dinosaur and allowed ourselves to be rescued. In the melee and confusion of being air-lifted back to Salt Lake, which proved to be the nearest city, Maximiliano Sacco and I faded back into the woodwork before any airline authorities or police could question us. Sacco was in a daze; he let me do the thinking for us both. All I had was a king-sized headache, a sprained back and a stiff leg but I had a billfold loaded with cash and travelers checks.

They would have to do.

For the little man and I were going to drop out of sight and lay low for awhile. So we would be moving targets, not sitting ducks.

That was what I wanted to do until I knew more about our predicament.

I never thought that my disappearance — or death as it turned out to be — would make morning headlines and bother a lot of people I loved and liked. But it gave Sacco and me the cover and protection we needed for the time being.

I had to know a helluva lot more about Walter Woody and Richard Roland before I dared surface again.

And then there was my attaché case. Left behind, on board the 747. What would the officials make of that?

But there was an even greater mystery than that.

A mind-boggler, a brain-wringer, an intellect-twister.

What was I doing talking to Maximiliano Sacco?

How could I be talking to Maximiliano Sacco?

Max, Max . . . who had died bloodily in my arms in flight somewhere high above the cockeyed universe . . . . *Or had he?*

Died with a mysterious knife jutting from his back like he was some new kind of dart board. *Sure, I'd seen all that . . . hadn't I? . . . HADN'T I?!!*

I stared up at the raging blue sky, the bursting ball of sun, and tried to still the boiler factory clanging in my skull. I couldn't. I was back in the desert again. The limitless wasteland, the buttes, the little man in the white suit . . . *Maximiliano Sacco . . .*

The old earth took a couple of whirls again. Mad, impossible, maniacal spins, taking me along for the ride.

And then the world exploded.

And I fell down.

All the way.
Deep, deep, deeper, deepest.
The Pits.
Maybe it was Eternity, maybe it was Hell.
But it was everlasting Nothingness.

8.

GOODBYE,
GARY COOPER

"How do you feel, Ed?"

"Crazy."

"What kind of crazy?"

"You know. Disoriented, out of it. Off the wall. It's like I'm outside myself, looking down at me, and laughing my head off."

"Why would you do that, Ed?"

"Why wouldn't I? We're all nuts, everything is whacko, out of sync. I mean — no two ends are meeting right. And everything is hazy and out of focus. Like a bad print of an old movie."

"Movies again. Always your frame of reference. That and sex. Did you ever wonder why your mind is like that?"

"I don't know. Dreams, I guess. Ideals, maybe, and hope. I wished for a lot in those darkened movie houses that throbbed when

I was a kid. And now — now it all seems so stupid and foolish."

"Why is it stupid and foolish, Ed?"

"Well, isn't it? How do you answer the simple truth that the Number One Cult Figure in all of the United States is a super bastard, stinker and just plain hateful character named J.R.?"

"That's just show business. A fad. A fancy. Public taste. It will pass."

"Sure it will but what does it say for the minds and hearts of the people who call this country home?"

"Not much, I agree. But it's only a condition. A manifestation. It's not logic or certainty or proof of anything."

"Doc, Doc. You're being evasive. And I'm the one who's supposed to be doing that. Don't switch parts on me, now. I'm loused up enough as it is. I'm running a pipeline to the nuthouse and if you don't stop me, if you can't — I'm out to lunch forever."

"You're too hard on yourself."

"Am I?"

"You are. No man is an island —"

"Don't John Donne me. But you're right. The bell is tolling. I hear it all the time now and that's the point. It is tolling for me."

"There you go. Movies again."

"That's right. Robert Jordan and Gary Cooper. Always Gary Cooper. My brain has been Cooper Territory since I was ten years old and he blew up that ammo dump in 'Bengal Lancers' after being machine-gunned across the back. Damn him."

"Damn Gary Cooper? Your God?"

"Yes. He made me believe in doing the right thing. In being a hero. In playing it straight. I've been a loser ever since."

"I wouldn't exactly call you that, Ed. World-famous private detective, healthy as a horse, still a free man in this day and age of IBM, machines and second-rate people —"

"Wouldn't you? I've got about five hundred bucks in the bank, no life insurance policy, no pension plan, no fringe benefits, no wife, no kids. Just a mouse auditorium of an office and I'm well past the bend in age. On the last turn —"

"Money and material things never meant anything to you. You said so. So why make it important now?"

"Because I haven't been working with a full deck lately. That's why. The plane crash, Maximiliano Sacco, the Woody thing — all that. How could it be so vivid to me? So real? When I know it didn't happen. Couldn't have happened. And yet — and yet — it's still with me. All of it. Every screwy second of it. I can still see him —"

"See who, Ed?"

"Max, Mike Monks — Melissa. Mel cried. Cried a lot when Mike told her . . . . It's all so damn weird. I can see it so plain."

"But you know it didn't happen. It was all an illusion. A dream. An unreality. You went on a mental trip. A bender, if you will."

"Yeah? I'll need a better explanation than that."

"I'm trying to give you one."

"Then full speed ahead, Doc. Where was I for two days if I wasn't on that plane? What was I doing and what did I say?"

"You won't like the answer."

"Like, shmike. I need the answer. I have to have it or I won't trust myself to go out and buy a pack of cigarettes anymore. Lay it on me, Doc. I'm a big boy. I can take it. All the way to the wall."

"Very well, then. Does the name Helen Hamlet mean anything to you?"

"Like in Shakespeare?"

"Like in Shakespeare. Eighteen years old, tall, long-haired. Black hair like midnight. As thin as a rail but very shapely. She's from Newburyport, Massachusetts and ran away from home last week to see New York and Times Square. That's where you found her or she found you."

"Go on."

"You registered as man and wife at the Essex House. One of your favorite hotels, isn't it? Well, that's where the police found you and her some time yesterday."

"Geezis."

"You had both been drinking. Something incredible. The police lab gave it a peculiar name but all that's important is that you and this Helen Hamlet became so intoxicated and wild that you set fire to the hotel room. One or both of you. You would both be dead now if a next-door guest hadn't acted fast. And properly. You and the girl were both taken to Roosevelt Hospital. They had to pump the girl. She was convulsing. And you — well, the report's on my desk — you kept saying names over and over again. One after the other: Dolores Ainsley, Alma Wheeler, Alberta Carstairs, Helen Tucker, Felicia Carr and Melissa Mercer. I'm sure you know who they are. I know. I asked Captain Monks. The only reason you're not cooling your heels in a police station now is because of him. But you are under observation and you must remain that way until I give you a clean bill of health."

"Never mind all that right now. What about this Helen Hamlet?"

"She died on the table. Bad heart. Complications."

"Geezis."

"Don't say that again. It indicates shock. You can't afford that now."

"But why would I do all that? What for? And my memory — of a jet and a murder and a case to work on, Walter Woody. Sacco . . . it happened, I tell you. It happened. It's all so vivid, so real —"

"Take it slow, Ed. Real slow. Let me talk. Confusion and protest only indicates fear. You'll unravel, box yourself into a corner. Let me talk. I do have an explanation. A partial one that makes sense. But it needs your cooperation and help. Now, don't talk. Just answer my questions. You'll see what I'm getting at soon enough. The girl is a victim of it, of course. But that's not your fault. The police also established that whatever it was you drank, it was in her clutch bag. That was one for your side. But registering at the hotel and the fire — well, we'll work that out too. Now, do you remember her at all? Very tall, very dark hair. Slender. Wearing Sasson jeans, three-quarter toggle coat. Scotch-plaid design. Three-inch spiked shoes. The jeans matched a blue silk shirt. She also wore a golden Star of David and a crucifix on one chain around her neck. No other jewelry. No rings. Her parents were notified but they have not showed up yet. It seems they're in Germany on a vacation."

"When did all this happen?"

"Yesterday. Twenty-four hours ago."

"All right. Go on. Tell me the rest of it."

"While the room was on fire and the next door guest broke in to save the two of you, he found you in a very strange state. The police report is very specific on that one point. The guest signed a sworn statement."

"You mean an affidavit, don't you, Doc?"

"Yes, *affidavit*. Why are you so careful about that word?"

"Just wanted to see if I remembered a tough word — the way I am now, I don't know anything for sure anymore. Go on. What was the strange state I was in?"

"You were completely naked. All of your clothes were neatly piled on the floor beside you. They were already smouldering and you were quite unaware. In fact, the guest said you were sitting on your haunches, Yoga-style you might say, talking your head off. It was sheer nonsense to him but his memory is precise — I have it down in the affidavit right here."

"What was I saying?"

"I'm quoting you now, exactly as the guest testified: *'Don't talk to him, Calamity!* . . .

*Bill Cody's with that ammunition train . . .
forty-eight men, Calamity! . . . Remember
what I told you. . . .'* You kept repeating
those words. Over and over again. Without
the slightest variation. Shouting them, then
whispering, then shouting again. The guest
also said your eyes were tightly shut, which
probably explains why you were paying no
attention to the fire or to Helen Hamlet. She
was also naked, by the way. But lying on her
stomach, arms outstretched, unconscious, in
one corner of the room. She was dying.''

"Geezis.''

"Meaning what, Ed?''

"Geezis, geezis, geezis!''

"What do those words mean, Ed — the
ones you kept repeating. Do you know what
they are, where they come from?''

"Do I know how to spell *Noon*? Ask me if I
know the color of my eyes or how many
fingers and toes I own! Oh, God — Cooper
again! Gary Cooper.''

"Would you please explain that?''

"Wild Bill Hickok and Calamity Jane.
Cooper and Jean Arthur. Another Cecil B. De
Mille history lesson, courtesy of the movies.
The Plainsman. Greatest western of them
all. Came out around thirty-seven and I've
seen it a hundred times since — those words
are Coop's lines when the Cheyenne are tor-
turing him over a slow fire to get Jean to spill
the beans about the direction the ammunition
train was heading. . . . *'Deep Valley. Through
the upper ford of the Republican. . . .'* ''

"That's very interesting, Ed.''

"Is it? I think it's Happydale talk, Looney

Tunes and get the Rubber Room ready for me. It told you — I'm working with half a deck."

"Steady, now. Let's take this one step at a time. We know your hang-up about Gary Cooper and heroism. You've been innoculated with it since you were a child."

"Nice try, Doc. Soothing. A real comfort. But I'm not buying it. What's your name, anyway? If it's Kildare or Welby the case is closed for me."

"Covington. Charles Covington. Charlie or Dr. Covington if you like."

"Okay, Charlie. Then that's it for me. I know now what I have to know."

"Now what do you mean?"

"Don't you see, Charlie? I've had it. All the way. I was in a plane crash that didn't really happen you say, I saw a man killed who wasn't really killed — you say — now you tell me I was in a burning hotel room with a young girl who died and I can't remember any of that at all — *what is real? What isn't?* Can't you see the writing on the wall, Dr. Charles Covington? The jig's up for me. Sherlock Holmes and Reichenbach Falls, Custer and Little Big Horn, Napoleon and Waterloo, Wild Bill Hickok and Aces And Eights — am I here in this all-white room? And better still, *are you*? Or are we both playing a scene from *Here Comes Mr. Jordan*? With you the Heavenly Messenger and me, filling in for Robert Montgomery — *Joe Pendleton*? You make a lousy Claude Rains, Covington. You haven't got his cultured whisper nor that old-smoothie manner."

"Take it easy, Ed."

"That's what I'm going to do, Doc."

"What are you picking up that chair for —"

"To hit you with, Doc. What else? I want out. And *now* — sorry, Doc. This just has to be done or I won't know anything anymore — and I'm tired of being afraid . . . damn tired . . ."

"Ed — don't!"

"Goodbye, Charlie. You were fun while you lasted."

Dr. Charles Covington was too large and too fat. And woefully out of condition, the way things turned out. He moved like molasses.

He never had a chance.

I hit him. Hit him hard. I think the chair splintered, hard as it was. Maybe hard enough to kill. I was past caring. Past knowing.

I was that far gone. Beyond. Over the rainbow.

And all I wanted to do, all I cared about at that exact moment in time, that pinpoint of Eternity, was to get away. To run, to hide.

The jackals were barking, the hell-hounds were screaming, the banshees were wailing, all the men with all the white nets were coming. The world was a solid, four-walled trap without windows.

But there was a door.

And I found it.

There's always a way out, an exit, if you really intend to use one. There was no one awake to pardon my dust.

Certainly not Dr. Charles Covington.

And this one time, leaving town was greater than Death.

9.

DID I KNOW
JEAN ARTHUR?

Later, much later, I don't know how much,
somewhere in Time, I found myself reading
something. A 4x6 index card held between
my fingers. A lamp behind me was throwing
a yellow light. There were dark shadows, a
lot of them, and all I could see was my two
hands holding the white index card. An
unlined, blank card, the kind you buy in a
stationery store. Librarians use them for fil-
ing book titles in the alphabet-marked
drawers, housewives write menus and
recipes on them and stick them in little metal
file boxes. What the hell was I doing with
them? I didn't know. I didn't know a lot of
things.

There was writing on this card, too.

Handwritten lines crowding the thing,
barely legible.

I strained to read the words, trying to

make some sense out of them, finally absorbing them — it wasn't easy. My mental processes were on vacation, loafing in the sun somewhere, refusing to work.

And the lines, the words themselves, were certainly no help to a confused, crazy, mixed-up man . . . . Dostoyevsky's *Idiot*.

Rapidly, the wand she held, now transformed into a deadly cobra — this nocturnal female was more than beauty could describe — beyond angelic — there wasn't a word in any dictionary to explain her radiance — splendor — elegance. St. G. knew she was evil — to the core of her lithe, lascivious body. Even while under her influence — mesmerised by his own reflections — how? How could such gorgeousness belong to the Devil? Then it struck him! Like a sharp razor blade! My God! Of course! Of course — the marble crucifix! That was it —

That's what was on the first side of the card. When I turned it over, I was no better off than I was before:

READ The Midnight Lady
    To The Devil — A Princess by Stephanie Kingsley.

I flung the card away. I cursed. Maybe I cried. I don't remember. Suddenly my hands came back into the light again and this time they held something else. A sheet of scrap paper, not much bigger than the card. I squinted down at it, unbelievingly. I was worse off than before:

It was two columns of figures, with four

headings and even as I read, the jackals and the hell-hounds and the banshees were having a field day. Ghouls-Night-Out:

PENNIES	QUARTERS
1942 S	1968 D
1947 S	1971 D
1948 S	1977 D
1949 D	1978 D
1950	1979 D
1950 D	
1954 S	**NICKELS**
1955 S	1962
1968 S	1962 D
1969 S	1963
1970 S	1965
1970 D	1976 D
1972 S	1978 D
1973 S	1980 D
	1981 D

DIMES
1976 D
1977 D

Geezis. Numismatically yours, Ed Noon . . . *why for God's sake?*

And geezis again. *And why again!*

I threw the scrap of paper away too. Into all that darkness that closed me in on four sides. I was alone again. Just me and the solitary yellow light. And my two hands. Uselessly, I stared down at them. I could still count ten fingers. That was something.

I tried to think. I couldn't.

I tried to laugh. I couldn't.

I tried to cry. I couldn't do that either.

Then suddenly, like magic, or an illusion, I was holding one more thing in my two hands. This time a letter-sized sheet of bond paper. I stared down at it foolishly. The lines blurred, telescoped, faded in and faded out. I shook my head. I blinked. I stared down.

In a world gone mad, a universe kaleidoscoping, I was the maddest hatter at the tea party. The looniest of the loonies. What my hands held, what my eyes saw was the final touch, the last stroke of leaping lunacy. Make Way For Crazy Eddie!

I was on a collision course with a moving nuthouse:

ITINERARY

Sept. 25   NEW YORK

Depart from New York from the Westside New Terminal Pier at 52nd Street to board the Mikhail Lermontov. Embarkation is from 9:30 AM and sailing is at 11:30 AM.

Sept. 25/Oct. 08

At sea.

Oct. 09/12   LENINGRAD

Arrive in Leningrad. Met and transferred to your hotel with first class accommodations and full board.

Oct. 13/16   LENINGRAD/MOSCOW

Transfer to the railroad station to board the Red Arrow Sleeper for Moscow.

Met and transferred to your hotel for first class accommodations.

Oct. 17/19   MOSCOW/KIEV

Transfer to the railroad station to depart from Moscow on train No. 21 departing at 12:35 PM and arriving in Kiev at 11:51 PM.

Met and transferred to your hotel for first class accommodations.

Oct. 20/23   KIEV/VINNITSA

Transfer to the Railroad Station to board your train No. 223 departing from Kiev at 5:29 PM and arriving in Vinnitsa at 9:21 PM. Met and transferred to your hotel. Note: Maximum stay is 6 days.

Oct. 24/28   VINNISTA/KISHINEV

Transfer to the railroad station to board train No. 85 to Kishinev. Approximate arrival in Kishinev is 10:25 AM. Met and transferred to your hotel.

Oct. 29   KISHINEV

Depart from Kishinev on the Danubius Express at 10:12 PM. Sleeping accommodations aboard the train.

Oct. 30/Nov. 03   BUCHAREST

Arrive in Bucharest at 7:41 AM. Met and transferred to the NORD HOTEL for accommodations.

Nov. 04   BUCHAREST

Transfer to railroad station to board the Danibus Express at 11:05 AM and arrive in Sofia at 6:48 PM. Change trains to the Istanbul Express for overnight accommodations.

Nov. 05/06   ISTANBUL

Arrive in Istanbul at 1:37 PM. Met and transferred to the HOTEL PERAPALOS for accommodations.

Nov. 07

OWN ARRANGEMENTS.

I stopped looking at my hands under the yellow light. I closed my eyes. Shut them hard against a world of insanity. And tried to think. It wasn't easy. The thoughts, the images, the ideas, all came slow, huffing, puffing, pulling themselves along like coupled freight cars struggling up a steep grade through the Rockies.

Names came to me, a veritable marching file of names. I let them come, let them parade before me, up front, where I could see them. I held them in check after they all assembled out of the chaos of my mind, bobbing up and down, so many corks on a troubled sea.

... *Maximiliano Sacco ... George Long ... Malvina . . . Miss Woodburn . . . Walter Woody ... Richard Roland ... Taft-Regent ... Winifred Roland ... Winifred Gentry ... Viviane Orley ... Paula Kluger ... Dr. Charles Covington . . . Helen Hamlet . . . Essex House . . . Fear Of Flying . . . jumbo jet ... Gary Cooper....*

I took them one-by-one, to restore some sense of order, of reason. I had to. The banshees, hell-hounds and jackals were whooping it up all over again and the Darkness was a solid, immovable thing.

An index card with purple prose scrawled on both sides.

A scrap of white paper with a listing of coins that only a collector would be interested in.

One printed itinerary for a trip to Russia, of all places.

Think, Noon, *think*, or it's all over for real this time.

I thought.

Sacco. Little man, white suit, no jewelry. On the plane. *"Kill Richard Roland for us, Mr. Noon. . . ."* No, that wasn't right. He said, *"Señor."* He always said *"Señor."*

Malvina. Stewardess. The 747. With a fanny that was a 10 from all directions. No more, no less.

Miss Woodburn. My fellow-passenger in flight from New York. The little old lady from Pasadena who had been a regular Jane Marple.

Walter Woody. The biggest myth since Howard Hughes. Maybe?

Richard Roland. A man who had written a book about Woody which might or might not be a hoax of king-size proportions.

Taft-Regent. Big publishing company, ready to do the Walter Woody Story for megabucks. Until sued by Woody's advisors, halting book publication . . . .

Winifred Gentry/Winifred Roland. The loving or unloving wife. Maybe blond, maybe brunette.

Viviane Orley. French model/health spa owner. The mistress or the joker in the whole deck of playing cards.

Paula Kluger. A faceless smart-ass who wrote bitchy letters. The lecture series at *Manhattan Criminal Investigation Department.*

I smiled out at the darkness, eyes closed and all. I was remembering details and long lists of names and all sorts of trivial things. A good sign. A very good sign . . . . I pushed on, trying not to sweat.

Dr. Charles Covington. Questions and answers in a hospital room somewhere. All that psychiatric mumbo-jumbo. I sincerely hoped I hadn't damaged him with the hard chair. Poor bastard. Trying to help me.

Helen Hamlet. The dead teen-ager found with me by the cops. I didn't remember a single thing about her. Shakespeare, anybody?

Essex House. Scene of the crime. The fire. The orgy. Whatever. My favorite hotel but what kind of proof was that?

Fear Of Flying. One worthless book. Miss Woodburn had been reading — a minor detail but solid evidence that my motor was running.

Jumbo jet. A bomb explosion. A power dive into the desert. All S.O.B.'s miraculously safe. Except Maximiliano Sacco and one Edward A. Noon. *How, why, where?* Covington said it was a nightmare, I had imagined the whole thing . . . then why did I know that *Mike Monks*, my one and only friend, had told *Melissa Mercer* that I was gone . . . ? It didn't add up . . . it didn't make sense . . . *be still my brain!*

Gary Cooper. Oh, yeah. And how. Never

forgetting him — no way. And me quoting all those lines from *The Plainsman*, that torture scene. Why the hell was that? Why that one . . . *and why now* . . . ? *I had to get out!*

I might have spoken out loud. Said all that over again.

For the answer came from somewhere out of that Darkness that walled me in on all sides. Came with all the mammoth importance and succinctness of God saying: *"Let there be light!"*

"You're not leaving town unless dead men can walk."

I did not dare open my eyes. *Wild Bill Hickok lived* —

There was no mistaking that tight-lipped, low, concise manner of speech. The laconic end-all of speakers. The ultimate Voice.

I waited, somehow knowing more was coming.

It came.

"The idea is still good, you know." Now it was *John Doe* —

My head pounded, my ears began to roar. Something was tom-tomming in my chest. Suddenly, there was no other sound in the whole wide world but that voice which I knew as well as my own, which I had heard so many thousands of times in darkened movie houses. That throbbed.

"You can't try too hard, Noon. You know that. Know it even better than I ever did . . . ." *Lou Gehrig and Longfellow Deeds* —

Now, the perspiration came. I felt it oozing, layering over me like the blanket of Death. I squirmed in the chair, struggled as if I were lashed to it with rawhide, which I wasn't.

"Go away," I moaned. "You're not real, you're not there . . . ."

"*Aren't I?*" the voice quietly mused. "*Says who? You?*"

"No — you can't be — you're dead — you died in May of nineteen sixty-one . . . cancer . . . . May the bad thirteenth . . . at three-twenty-seven p.m. . . ."

"*Maybe so. But I'm still alive for the likes of you. I always will be. I'll never die because you never wanted me to. That's pretty powerful stuff, Noon. The Greeks had a word for it. Mythology.*"

"Oh, geeziz . . . it can't be . . . *it can't!* . . . ."

"*Can't it, Ed?*" The oh-so-well-loved voice was softer now. "*Open your eyes and see, huh? The two-gun plainsman is back. Your own Beau Geste. . . . Robert Jordan. The Pride of the Yankees. Sergeant York. The White Knight . . . come on, Noon. Before Frank Miller gets off the noon train to meet those gunnies that are waiting for him. Then he's going to come gunning for me. And you. All over again. Just like he always will. Just like they always will.*"

"Who, for God's sake!" The cry blurted out of me like a shotgun blast. "Who are you talking about — ?"

"*The Bad Guys. The Villains. The Louses. The Four-Star Rats who will always want to take over. The ones you always saw me fight and rooted for me to beat. Same as you been doing all of your grown life, Ed Noon. Open your eyes and say hello to an old friend. I wish we'd met in real life. Guess it didn't matter then. But it does now. If you'll open your eyes and look at me so I can see the expression in your face, when I tell you, then you'll understand why. Okay?"*

I took a deep breath. It seemed like a year to do. *Breathe.*

"Okay —"

"Good. I'm not anything frightening, you know. I'm still me."

"You swear?" I whispered, awed, terrified, no matter what he said. My brain was on fire. "Like you made Walter Brennan swear on a lock of Lily Langtry's hair in *The Westerner?"*

There was a pause. Heavenly or hellish, I couldn't say.

"I swear," came the quiet, authoritative pledge. *"This is one true thing, General Yang."*

I opened my eyes, slowly.

There was no more darkness, no more light. The solitary yellow bulb was gone. There was only a tall, elegantly lanky figure standing before me, no more than five feet off from the Emerald City, El Dorado and Shangri-la. A figure fit to occupy all those places. Xanadu, too.

He was as I remembered him, as I never could forget him, togged out in the belted trenchcoat, the flyer's jodphurs and the slick, trim fedora slanted across his one-of-a-kind face. The O'Hara costume from Milestone's unforgettable *The General Died At Dawn.* Soldier-of-Fortune O'Hara, perhaps the pluperfect kind of role for an actor that

looked like he had, that had been as he had
been. No one had ever looked better.

"Hello, Gary Cooper," I said, no longer
afraid, oddly at peace. "Long time no see.
Where were you when I needed you?"

The marvelous grin, the one that was all
warmth and sincerity, flashed before me, as
vital and alive as ever. Magical film rolled.

"So you know me then — that's *good.*"

"Know you?" I echoed foolishly. "Did I
know Jean Arthur?"

"Yeah, you knew her all right. Just like
you knew Dolores Ainsley, Alma Wheeler,
Alberta Carstairs, Helen Tucker, Felicia
Carr and Melissa Mercer . . . . But this is different, Ed. Way different."

"How different?" I parried, still marveling
at seeing him again, watching him up close,
somehow knowing that he wasn't dead and
incredibly, not asking the miracle for any
more references.

Gary Cooper's grim tight smile was
Michael Geste's death grin on the sandy
floor of Fort Zinderneuf. Without the bugle
blowing.

"This isn't only Hadleyville and High
Noon, Ed — it's the end of the universe. The
Great Big Last Bang. And you've got to
stop it — before it stops everything else."

"Stop what?"

"Force Five from Up There Somewhere."

I blinked at that. I had to. I didn't understand him at all.

"Run that by me again —"

His spatulate forefinger poked upward,
timed with an eloquent shrug of his

shoulders. His voice fell to a quieter level. Now it was the only sound in the world. The universe.

"It's come at last, Ed — what everyone has been wondering about for centuries. There *is* Life up there and they've finally made up their collective minds to come. To come down. Invade. Take over. And it all began with the creation of one legendary human being named Walter Woody — keep your seat. Don't get up. I'll tell you the whole thing. And it won't be like anything you ever saw at a Saturday matinee at the Ritz Theatre in your dear old Bronx."

"Say I swear to God," I begged, foolishly.

Gary Cooper smiled again. A Christ-on-the-Cross-like smile.

"I swear to God."

So I listened. I had to do that, too. As rapt as any child hearing his parent talk about Santa Claus and Christmas. Or Evil and the Devil. You always listen to your Gods.

And Cooper had been mine.

On this earth and in this world — at least.

Nobody had ever played the part better. Not like The Ace had.

He was also the father I had never known.

Detective Sergeant Thomas Anthony Noon had been shot down in the line of duty while my mother was still carrying me. Way back there in the dark ages of the Twenties — 1927, to be exact.

So Gary Cooper spoke.

And I listened.

10.

STAR TRACK

"There is no Walter Woody, Ed. There never was. He was a creation, a name, a powerful figure. Something like a front for all the big deals, the manipulations, the scams that this alien force from up yonder needed to get their plan started. And to keep it in operation."

"Something like Howard Hughes?"

"Yes. But of course there was a Hughes. A genius of aviation and wheeling-and-dealing who built up an empire worth billions over forty years. But —" The darkness of the room somehow was under a halo, a nimbus of light so that the only thing visible was the tall, lanky, well-loved form. "Just like the Clifford Irving thing — you know, he wrote a phony book and Howard Hughes, Man of Mystery, finally surfaced to put the kibosh on the whole hoax. Well, this Richard Roland character decided to try the same thing on the legend everybody knew as Walter Woody. The biggest difference was that he didn't know he was going up against an invisible empire. A line of alien minds and creatures who long ago had decided to begin their take-over of this planet we call Earth —"

"This Force Five outfit you mentioned . . . ."

"Yes. But more about them later." The tight grin grimmed-up again. "You can see where they were at. Sitting on a big needle. The whole scheme of a Walter Woody exposure was too tricky, too loaded with possible chances of the master plan going up. So, their next step was to discredit this Roland, just like the real Hughes did to Irving, making him out to be no more than a very clever liar and bunco artist. Yet, that wasn't enough. Eliminating Richard Roland was more the ticket. The insurance. So, they thought of finding an expert, a perfect professional. One who could be relied on to stop the clock of Richard Roland forever. In that way, the Force Five Plan for the world could go on uninterrupted, with no hitches. They could keep buying up oil fields, oceans of real estate, gasoline refineries, big hotels, conglomerates — every kind of public utility — the sort of big operation that would never make necessary the use of an atom bomb or lasers or masers or any kind of hardware to dominate the territory known as the United States. You following all this, Ed?"

"I never was much for science fiction but go on, please."

"So they knew you were going on a plane ride. So they put Maximiliano Sacco on your trail. And he made you the offer —"

I held up both hands. "Whoa — slow down. You're telling me I was the expert, the Top Pro, they wanted to put Richard Roland out of commission?"

"That's it. He offered you a million dollars, didn't he?"

Images collided, scenes reeled, lap dissolves of Sacco, the plane, the bursting explosion, the power dive, the walk in a Western nowhere, the hospital, Dr. Charles Covington, the dead teenager — I was thoroughly rattled now. Yanking my head back and forth, trying to make some sense out of all of this.

"I know what you're thinking, Ed."

I smiled wanly. "You do? Then tell me."

"You're wondering about Sacco. Man or creature? Well, you are right. The little man was an android. Cloned to look like a little man in trouble. He could not come to you as he really is. So he came in human form. Force Five creatures are not something I can describe to you. They're like horrible creations out of H. P. Lovecraft."

"Miss Woodburn would have screamed at the sight of him, huh?"

"She would have jumped through the nearest plexiglass window. You understand — Sacco had you almost convinced — and then something unforeseen developed. Something even the android named Maximiliano Sacco could not have counted on.

Something that had nothing to do with Sacco or Force Five's plans for you in the Richard Roland matter."

"Explain." That was more Kirk than Noon but I couldn't help it. I needed all of Mr. Spock's logic to follow what I was hearing. Gary Cooper or no Gary Cooper. There was a limit, *somewhere*.

"There was a bomb on board that plane. Planted by a suicidal fanatic who was determined to blow himself and everybody else up. Sacco came upon him just as he had wired a home-made device — manufactured while the 747 was in flight — so he stabbed Sacco and completed his explosive. Sacco misunderstood the attack. He thought it was Richard Roland-inspired — friends of Roland out to stop him from contacting you. You know the rest. The bomb blew, the nose disintegrated and the pilot made a miracle landing . . . ." Gary Cooper shrugged, again.

My brain halted. I tried not to blink. The room, if it was a room, was like a vacuum. I felt smothered in layers of cotton. There was no sound save the quiet, clipped voice talking to me. But somewhere in all that nowhere was the pounding conviction inside me that all of this wasn't quite right. Was incorrect. Did Gods lie to you? Did they tell you things just to kiss it and make it well? I fought back, shaking my head. I must have looked like a rag doll without coordination of any kind.

"No —" I protested. "I don't know the rest. Sacco was killed on that plane. Died on the spot right in front of me. And then we were walking among the buttes as nice as you please — come on, Gary. Give me a break. Covington said I dreamed the whole thing — and now you're telling me there was a plane crash, after all."

"You still don't understand, do you?"

"No, I don't."

"Haven't you been listening? Sacco was an android. Is an android. They don't die. They can't. They can only be put out of commission. Temporarily. The knife blade only short-circuited him. A minor mishap. Back on the ground, he repaired himself and took care of you — Covington is one of them, Ed. He told you a lot of lies to keep you calmed down. Can't you see that?"

"No, I can't. All this sci-fi hogwash is out of my league. They walk through walls, they materialize and de-materialize — Christ! If they have all that power, why bother with Richard Roland? Or me? Shoot us or stab us or put poison in our coffee but why in hell all this maneuvering and plotting and planning? It just doesn't make sense. No sense at all, G.C. Just like me sitting here talking to you, as if you really did come back to life, is the biggest trolley ride to the Laughing Academy there ever was. It's Funny Farm Time and I must be dead myself and this is some kind of idea what my Hell, if there is a Hell, is going to be like. Crazy plots, old movie stars, a million remembered pieces of film business, a whole army of quotations and God only knows what else — Help — I'm drowning, Coop. Go away. Lap dissolve, vanish and leave this old corpse in peace. I've had enough. I haven't even thought of

Melissa Mercer and making love — or love at all. And that's not me. So, Dreadful Apparition, why do you haunt me so? Now you got me quoting Dickens —"

"Ed, you are not dead."

"Prove it."

"All right. I will."

I never expected what came next. I never saw it, either. His hard right hand, bunched into a fist, zoomed out from his shoulder and made direct contact with my chin. The chair and I went over backwards with a slam of sound. I came up, blinking hard. The right side of my jaw throbbed with pain. Agony. But it was a sensation. A reaction to a force. And dead men can't feel punches.

"Sorry, Ed," the voice floated over me, somewhere. "You felt that didn't you?"

"Just like Mr. Cedar in the courtroom in *Mr. Deeds*," I agreed, very, very slowly righting the chair and sitting down in it again. "And Tom Tyler and Forrest Tucker and Bill 'Stage' Boyd and Lloyd Bridges and Henry Wilcoxon and that nameless Indian extra in *The Plainsman* —" That got the tent smile from *Wings* out of him.

"You'll be all right. Once you start reeling off film bits, I know your think-box is working. Okay, then. Where were we?"

"Still on a fantasy flight but — all right — I'll play. You keep talking and I'll keep listening. But who's *Them*?"

"Force Five's traditional enemies. The Bardons. Rival planet. They too want to get in on this Take-Over-The-Earth thing. Covington had to keep you off-stride while he tried to learn what you know."

"Then, all that stuff about Helen Hamlet, the Essex House and her being dead was —"

"Hokum. All of it. It never happened."

"Covington an Alien, too?"

"Yep. You never could have guessed that. Not the condition you were in. The chair you hit him with put him down, all right. But that's all. The idea was to mix you up, anyway. Find out what you really knew about Sacco. These Bardons are out for blood. The whole ballgame. Believe it or not, Ed Noon."

I laughed. A brittle, humorless laugh.

"You think all this is funny, Ed?"

"A scream. From the top to the bottom line." I made like a parrot. " *The only thing necessary for the triumph of Evil is for good men to do nothing . . . .'* Unquote. Am I a good man?"

"The best. A real genuine old-fashioned model. That's why I'm here. That's why you're sitting there listening to me. You're the one to handle this Force Five scare. Nobody else could because nobody else would swallow all this. Understood?"

"I hear you talking, G.C."

"Good." He seemed to relax for the first time, nodding.

"So just like you did, and always did, I'm to go up against Trampas, Mohamet Khan, John Lattimer, Sergeant Markoff, D.B. Norton, Ellsworth Touhey and Frank Miller — all those villains and guys like that. Only you call them Force Five and Bardons. Geezis."

"Yes. And your target is one Richard Roland. Stop him, liquidate him. The way Sacco asked you to."

"Hit Man From Outer Space. Is that it?"

"That's it. You got it." Suddenly, the tall figure before me began to evanesce, to glow and shimmer. The white trenchcoat, the jodphurs, the boots dimmed. The one-of-a-kind face under the snappy fedora seemed to lose color, to ebb. When they made that face, they threw away the mold but I started to panic again. I tried to get up from the chair. I couldn't. My feet were suddenly cemented to the floor. The Coop voice came back, though fainter than before. "I've got to go now. But I'll be back. When you need me. But right now, you're on your own . . . ." It was a Cheshire Cat vanishing act.

"But where am I?" I shouted, my heart climbing to my mouth. "What day is this — what year — I haven't any money — no gun — I'm lost — give me a break, Gary, you gotta tell me more so I'll know where to begin . . . ."

"At the beginning, Ed. And forget that scrap of paper and the coin list and the Russian itinerary. Covington planted those on you just to confuse you even more — remember? I'm with you in this. All the way . . . take care . . . and good luck . . . . *Get Richard Roland* . . . ."

Poof! He was gone. The lone yellow bulb shone down on empty space again. With the same old darkness beyond. I rose from the chair then and my feet came away free. I was light, airless, walking on the moon. My mind rioted, the five senses I owned all doing a mad polka. Damn it, I heard music too. Steiner out of Korngold out of John Williams. And it was like the scores of *King Kong* and *Robin Hood* crossed with *Star Wars* and *Raiders Of The Lost Ark*. And incredibly, madly, it all segued into the funeral cortége music from *Lost Horizon*. Dmitri Tiomkin triumphant — but my High Lama had vanished as quickly and magically as he had come. And now, I was alone one more time.

All alone. Just me and my nightmare. My madness. I, One Man.

As solitary and isolated as the needle in the haystack, the single cherry atop a mammoth cake, the lone bulb in a blacked-out stretch of The Great White Way, Broadway. Or was I but a single star in the great galaxy of the Milky Way?

I didn't know. I would never know. Somehow, I was sure of that.

I hadn't been brain-washed. No, not at all. My brain had been removed, thoroughly picked apart, put together again and then been replaced in my skull. But nothing was working. Everybody was out to lunch . . . and I had done something only the TV shows talk about.

I had gone where no man had ever gone before.

Beyond.

There's no place in this wacky universe more far out than that.

Ask the crew of the Starship *Enterprise*.

But worse than that, I was living a Martian Chronicle.

So help me, Ray Bradbury.

11.

BASS ACKWARDS

They weren't through with me yet. Whoever they were, whatever they were. No way in heaven or hell. No sooner had the ghost or the dream or the nightmare of The Late But Great Gary Cooper come and gone than they were at me again. All over me.

Women this time. More than one. Blond, brunette, slender, full, dream woman and bitch altogether. I tried to get away from them, roll off their damp, pulsating bodies but it was no use. I was trapped. Plastered to them, pushing down at them, all wrapped about them, trying to hold on, hang on, fuck on. Oh, geezis — where was I? What was I doing — *Oh, Gary Where Art Thou?*

"There's something awfully chemical about you, Ed. I get vibrations . . . ."

"Don't mess with me, Tucker. I can be unforgettable."

Helen Tucker. Broadway agent. Murderess. A dream lost and left behind over thirty years ago. Turned over to the cops by Yours Truly in the best Bogart-Sam Spade tradition. Where was she now — still cooling her heels in prison? Or long since paroled? I didn't know and I never found out, either. Damn me.

"Ed Noon — Christ, what a big mouth you are! Don't you ever stop talking? You must have icewater in your veins."

That was Dolores Ainsley. The Tall Dolores. Alma Wheeler's murderous sister. I had killed Dolores accidentally while she bolted down the flight of steps in the Statue of Liberty. No, we had never made love but I had thought about it — she had been titanic.

"Old magic mouth — Ed, you're something, you know it?"

"Shut up, Wheeler, and kiss me."

Alma. Blond, beautiful, altogether unique. The one-of-a-kind woman. Reformed Call Girl and the One That Got Away.

And then there was Alberta Carstairs, the smooth sophisticate, the *Now* woman of Gloria, Incorporated, the great clothing line.

"Love me, Ed. Please love me — I've waited for you a long time."

"Sure you have, Carstairs. Forgive me, Alberta —"

Roaring, heaving interludes with all of them. Scenes from a Very Great Movie. Quiet whispers in the dark. Touch, sound, feel, smell, taste — a million and one glorious sensations — hot, hot lips.

Then Melissa Mercer walks in. More than

a secretary. Midnight lady. The darker love. The Diahann Carroll clone. The common sense, the pithiness, the sharp, true sound of her. Black Beauty, Inc.

"*You phony, you. All big and tough on the outside. Inside, just one little boy.*"

"No boy ever had what I have, Mel. Come here, you."

She came. She had kept on coming. And all the time I was going in and out of her life like a boomerang. First alive, then dead, then alive again — and sometimes double-crossing her. All unwillingly. No, that's not right. I was willing but the results were unintentional.

Like Felicia Carr. Naval Intelligence. Government Girl. Lean, a willow tree, hair the color of black ink. Another damsel in distress circling my world of improbability. The Doomsday Bag lady.

"*You did it, Ed. Like you said you would. Up there — way up there you took me — and brought me down again. Safe —*"

"It's easy to do when the woman looks like you — is you."

All the pretty speeches I had made, all the promises, all the wolf songs I had sung in pursuit of the crazy urges which bulge a man's crotch. What was real, what was not real? Better than that, what was the truth, Doubting Thomas? And please stay for the answer.

And now — I groaned, pushing out, smashing at the lovely faces hovering, crowding me in. *Helen, Dolores, Alma, Alberta, Melissa, Felicia.* Their sad eyes were accusing. Mocking — "*Go away,*" I was begging now. "*Leave me alone — I'm dead — I can't do anything for you! My ticket's punched, I've bought the farm, I've gone West — it's Lights Out, Curtains, The Last Round-Up — Kaput! Jesus H. Christ, don't any of you understand English —* I'M DEAD! DEAD, DEAD, DEAD!"

They finally understood.

They all disappeared in a thunderclap of sound.

And the Silence was louder than ever.

It didn't help. Didn't help at all. A veritable roll-call of names seemed to echo in my ears . . . names of ladies from all the cases I had ever been mixed up in, ladies who had mixed me up too, a lot of might-have-beens who had gone back to their own lives and pasts after walking into mine. *April Wexler, Mimi Tango, Lois Hunt, Opal Trace, Peg Temple, Ilsa Dorn, Penny Darnell, Violet Paris, Rita Riker, Helen Friday — be still, my brain! — Terry Ricco, Holly Hill —*

The world around me widened, narrowed, expanded and then popped like a cork. All darkness and changing colors faded. The lone yellow light bulb disappeared. So did the chair I sat on. And whatever room, cell or nuthouse I was occupying. Suddenly, I was in bed. In a very, very fine room somewhere. A room with a view. Beyond a huge picture window I saw the canyons and twinkling lights of Los Angeles. It had to be L.A. I recognized the view from the time of the B.Z. Murder Case. When Violet Paris had put out the lights of Bennett Zangdorfer forever for the crime of being One Dirty Old Man. Vivacious, incomparable Violet had told me I looked like William Holden. But that was before I started looking like a re-conditioned Gene Kelly.

I felt fine all of a sudden. Mint condition. In the pink.

Just like that. Quick as a bunny.

No pain, no agonies, no bad or sad memories. It was Euphoria, Exaltation and What Me, Worry? Everything I had thought about or considered recently was all gone. Someone had Made Nice.

And the bed and the room — one was deep, mountainously pillowed, silk-sheeted and my naked body was settled down like an olive in a delicious martini — and the other was cool, delightful and altogether tophole. I was on Easy Street. Seventh Heaven without hooks. I hadn't a care in the world. Not even a notion about the Fate of the Universe. I would have gotten Walter Woody confused with Woody Woodpecker if I had been asked right then and there.

I wasn't asked.

I was shown.

There was a woman in the room with me. In the bed with me.

I didn't see her at first, being all involved with the view of Los Angeles at night from the bed, that and the room and its lush and supra-pleasant environs. And then I saw her. All at once. Like a flash of lightning across a midnight sky. A sexual thunderbolt.

She was standing at the foot of the bed, staring down at me, both hands resting on glowing, bell-shaped hips. She was naked, too. But that was really the last thing I noticed about her. Everything else commanded my attention first.

That same lightning must have struck her hair. It was a bursting, exploding profusion of blond rays. Golden, dazzling, spilling to her shoulders, framing an oval face whose eyes gleamed down at me almost metalically, like the eyes painted on those headboards of video traps in the Fun and Games arcade parlors. A copy of the Bride of Frankenstein, maybe, only this one was a Knockout. A Ten in any Computer League. Her breasts were contoured hills. Firm, round, full, the exquisite nipples crested the mounds. The wicked dimple of the navel winked at me above a perfectly triangular veldt of pubic glory. She stood straddle-legged, and the determination and willfulness of that posture alone was enough to make me remember why I had been born. The skin and flesh of her body might have been Essence of Honey. There was a lambent aura around her, too. There was no doubt at all about the heat she exuded. Her gorgeous, chiseled, sensuous face was incredible.

Very few women have ever looked like that.

Maybe Ursula Andress, Julie Christie or Sophia Loren — it's a vulgar, passionate look. The kind all women turn on in private but only very few wear publicly. You know what I mean — pagan, buddy, strictly pagan.

The glittering eyes seemed to laser down at me.

Even they gave off a Fahrenheit 451. *Julie Baby* . . . .

"I am Halina," she said. Low, quiet. But it might have been a machine talking. A sexy, one, of course — a distaff Hal right out of *2001, A Space Odyssey.*

"Of course," I agreed. "No other name would suit you. Who the hell else could you be?"

"That is what I am called, Edward."

"We've established that already, Halina. Why are you here or more to the point — what have you come to me for?"

"My instructions are to gratify all of your sexual requests."

"Do tell. Suppose I don't have any?"

"That is not possible. I have been briefed on your case history. You are a thoroughly sexually-oriented carbon unit. As well as a Hollywood mental product."

"My, my. All that? Little Old Me. They got me down in the records, huh? What else have they got?"

"I have not been programmed for anything else, Edward."

"That's a relief."

"I do not understand that remark. Is it Positive or Negative?"

"Negative, Sister. Strictly Negative."

"You are confusing me, Edward. We are not related. We could not be. I am the product of the mating union of a male and female Bardon. A carbon-unit offspring would not be scientifically possible."

I shut my eyes, holding back an inner groan. I opened them again. It was no use. She did not evaporate or go away. She was still there. Every shimmering, bountiful, sense-shattering atom of her.

"Halina, tell me something — please —"

The quiet, uninflected feminine voice did not lose patience with me.

"You are the Master here. You do not have to beg. I will tell you anything and all that I am capable of telling."

"What is Force Five?"

"I do not know of any such designation."

"But you're a Bardon. You must know. Aren't they your enemies? Aren't you both trying to take over the Earth? World Domination and all that crap all over again — like Gary Cooper told me."

"I do not know what you are talking about, Edward. May I suggest we deal with the situation I was designed for?"

I was talking to a robot. An android. A Whatever. And I had nothing to fight with, being completely insane, uprooted and far, far from the madding crowd and the life I knew so well. I sagged against the mountainous pillows, flung aside the silken sheets that covered my nakedness and gestured downward wildly.

"Of course — why the hell not? Damn the torpedoes, full speed ahead — go ahead, Halina — fuck me, fuck me good — feel free. Be my guest. Westward, Ho!!!!!!!! You little old Clockwork Orange you!"

"Yes, Edward. I will do as you say."

"Go ahead. Say it, damn you!"

She bent at the waist, kneeled to the foot of the bed and came toward me. The electric-like eyes glittered strangely. The bold, red slash of a full mouth opened. White teeth dazzled. A pink tongue slithered over her lips. There was a scent of jasmine in the air.

"Yes, Edward. I will fuck you. I have been instructed in all the strange words and lexicon and jargon of carbon-units that are used during the act of coupling. I shall not disappoint you."

"You damn-well better not. Or I'll send you back to the factory for maintenance. And a new set of springs, my stainless steel Halina. Didn't I see this in *Barbarella*?"

I was wrong. It was a mattress session out of Fantasyland. Something all growing boys dream about but seldom ever find because it was never real to begin with. Only something imagined. Something longed and hoped for. Something always impossible to achieve because the concept of such a thing is wrong in the first place. In the second, it can never be what the female wants it to be, either. Her dreams are even wilder than ours.

But not Halina's. Halina, the manufactured playgirl, designed and programmed for orgy and sexual satisfaction, clicked on all six cylinders, eighteen rheostats or whatever the hell she was composed of — Halina went to town on me. With a bucket of wanton paint, a dish of jollies, a mouth, and a Delta Triangle that had to be gifts from Hell. Heaven could not hold a Halina. She would have been useless there.

I didn't fuck her.

She fucked me. *For Unlawful Carnal Knowledge* — from Outer Space.

There is a difference.

How did she love me?

Let me tell you the ways . . . .

"Are you pleased, Edward?"

"Halina, please."

"May I ask a question, Edward?"

"Mmmmmm . . . ."

"Is that acquiesence, Edward?"

"Yes, damn you — yes!"

"Why is it that when I place my tongue about your biological device and taste you that you react with so much pleasure? Is it as much of a stimulus as your actions suggest?"

"Oh, you figure it out, huh?"

"I will try. For myself, it is merely a function. Yet I must confess to a certain curiosity."

"Such as — ?"

"When I position myself beneath you and widen my opening to receive you and you maintain that upward and downward movement with such continued regularity, I admit there is a certain well-oiled smoothness and pleasantness to the rhythm. My inner recesses seem to expand and contract in time with your motions."

"And then — ?"

"I do not understand you, Edward."

"I mean — what happens to you then? What happened then?"

"I do not know. Suddenly, you stopped. There was that small explosion. Your juices filled me. You then subsided. You said nothing, but the pleased expression on your face told me I had satisfied some craving within you."

"Check and double-check."

"Check? You did not write anything, Edward — ?"

"Forget it. I have to remember who you are, what you are and why you are here. And who sent you — though Christ only knows what this is all about and where it will all truly end. I expect to wake up any old minute now. Safe and sound in a rubber room somewhere in Happydale. That will be the only thing that will make sense . . . . I may have the stick that does the trick, but you, you're Something Else. Tell me, Halina — when does this LSD trip end for me? When can I go back home again? To the Mouse Auditorium and sweet sanity. There's a black angel I want to see again and an old tired cop with a face like bum shoe leather. I don't care anymore about Maximiliano Sacco and Walter Woody and the fate of Mankind. I'm tired. More tired than I have ever known —"

She raised her lovely, chiseled face from the vicinity of the family jewels and paused. Something like a puzzled look showed in the electric-light deep, dark eyes. The pink tongue withdrew once more behind the blood-red lips. She was still drinking me.

"You can return to what you desire, and what you truly want, anytime you are ready, Edward."

"Please repeat that once more."

"I do not understand your bewilderment. You have always been able to go back to where you came from. I thought you understood that. It is one of the conditions of your complex behavior patterns. You are not a prisoner here. You never have been."

I cursed. "Who is Number One? Oh, geezis —"

"There is no Number One. We are all individual yet a part of the whole. It is the plan and order of our cosmos. We serve each other. No one rules."

She crouched, draped above me, those splendid mammaries still suspended close by. Her golden hair hung about her oval face like a mushroom cloud. There was no escape, no matter what she was saying. I was hooked into Movieland and my own madness as surely as there were five Dionne Quintuplets, Seven Lively Arts, and Six Black Horses for every old funeral in the West of long ago.

"Why do you smile, Edward? It is a very strange smile for I see no amusement in it. Only sadness."

I turned my face from her and stared at the far wall of the very pleasant room that now seemed all prison, all confinement, all entrapment. "I am sad. Little Dorothy who got lost in Oz and then found out she could go back to the farm in Kansas anytime she had wanted to. She didn't need the Wonderful Wizard or the Scarecrow or the Tin Man or the Cowardly Lion. She had the key all the time — she just didn't know she had it. Or how to use it."

Halina lifted herself from me, glided away and then stationed herself at the foot of the bed again. Her posture was tall, erect. Only the outlandishly perfect curves and contours of a body right off an artist's drawing board gave the lie to her machinery. Her consummate dimensions. She stared down at me. The deep, dark eyes glowed. The superb breasts rose like the shoreline at Big Sur.

"You have the key, Edward. And I have accomplished my assignment. You are ready now to go back. Your mind and your will are free once more."

"Oh, yeah. Where is the key?"

"In your head where it has always been. You may use it whenever you want. It has been a pleasure servicing you, Edward."

Behind her, I saw the twinkling lights of Los Angeles, stabbing the darkened night sky. There was a subtle change in things, a gradual lessening of all colors, objects, shapes. Halina began to shimmer, sway, her outline fanning out, dissolving. The Cooper routine I had been put through already. I tried to rise to a sitting position. I threw my arms out, trying to halt the vanishing act.

"Hey, wait — you inter-galactic call girl! I still don't know about a lot of things — *Halina! For God's sake, don't go!*"

Not for me, or Him, or anybody else, could Halina stop what she was doing. What was happening. All at once, she was gone. With no noise, no shower of sparks, no fiery burst of light. No anything. She had vanished into the Void. And so had the room, Los Angeles and everything else that surrounded me.

There was no warmth or coldness, no light, no dark, no temperature change — no nothing. If there is a Fourth Dimension and it is Time, I had lost that, too.

The Theory of Relativity had always eluded me. Any number higher than a thousand had always given me trouble. And now — I was adrift again in that same old sea of madness and insensate nightmaring that had brought me to where I now was — Little Eye Lost. Real lost.

Come Back, Little Shamus —

Afraid, I closed my eyes again. Tight. Just like Dorothy of Kansas. I didn't say over and over again, *"There's no place like the Mouse Auditorium —"* but I was thinking that just the same. *Hard.*

Later, I don't know how much later, I forced my eyes open.

Sunlight flooded an office. A Vitamin D explosion.

There was a four-drawer Cole file, a contour chair and a deeply-grained mahogany desk. The wide picture window faced Manhattan skyscrapers. I stared down at myself.

Saw a Brooks Brothers suit, a blue foulard tie, a white shirt and nice Italian *Roma* black shoes. My legs were crossed. I was sitting back in the contour chair. I swiveled in it, turning to face the connecting door that led out to the receptionist's office.

It was a place I had been before.

A place that was the only real home I had ever known since St. Thomas' Protectory in the Bronx, a lifetime ago. Thomas Anthony

Noon's line-of-duty death and the subsequent loss of my mother had made me an orphan at twelve. Something I hadn't thought about in forty years — you can't count the Army as Home.

The place warmed me, thrilled me. Unbidden, tears came to my eyes. I let them fall, not caring, not giving one good goddamn about what it must have looked like. I was home again.

Home.

I was sitting in the Mouse Auditorium.

Somewhere over the Rainbow.

A lovely place where there was no room for Maximiliano Sacco, Walter Woody, Mrs. Woodburn, Malvina, Richard Roland, Dr. Charles Covington or Halina. Not even for Gary Cooper. Sorry about that, Ace.

ED NOON PRIVATE INVESTIGATIONS. Owner and Sole Proprietor.

Damn. The drinks were on me.

The world was right-side up again.

12.

HI, NOON — WHERE THE HELL HAVE YOU BEEN?

I walked out to Melissa Mercer's desk.

She was not there. The clothing tree by the front door held only my pork-pie fedora, the grey one I have worn down to a frazzle in fair weather and foul, running gun fights and general roughhouse. There was a tiny chrome clock on the Mercer desk. It said 1:55, in digital certainty. Everything was numbers these days. The computers have taken over. I checked the Seiko on my left wrist. It said the same thing, also in digits. Everything was evening out. I stared down at the THINGS TO DO TODAY pad on Melissa's desk. There was a message there for me, in her own fine hand.

Something inside me calmed down though I felt like letting out three ringing cheers. Mel's communique said nothing about blown-up 747's, the death of Ed Noon or even a Where-You-Been, Lover?

It was all so childishly simple. Business as usual:

Gone to Chase to deposit those checks. No calls. I'll pick up a card for Mike. His birthday is Friday — the first. We'll decide on a present for him when I get back — Love ya, Boss Man.

Melissa

I turned from the message to the calendar on her desk. When my eyes saw the big red letters 26 and the heading FEBRUARY 1988, my breath sucked in. Slowly coming around, the Norman Rockwell calendar on the wall, the large reprint of his baseball-game-interrupted-by-rain scene, hit me right between the eyes. FEBRUARY 1988 mocked me again. I had lost six whole months somewhere in the middle of that mental roller-coaster ride I had just taken. I was away someplace in my own personal Twilight Zone. Or was it just a simple case of amnesia? I didn't know. I didn't know anything anymore.

Gone was the euphoric feeling. The sense of joy and release. Doubts came thundering back, a herd of wild buffalo stampeding around in my brain. I went back into my office, flopped down on the contoured armchair and sat back and brooded. A long, long time.

When Melissa Mercer came gliding in, with her easy, well-coordinated stride, that was how she found me. Staring up at the ceiling as if I was considering having a new sprinkler system installed. I was really thinking about having a brain transplant. I was thoroughly disoriented again.

"Hi, Noon," she said in that throaty blues-singer voice of hers. "From the picture of the same name. Been back long, Ed?"

"Half-hour, hour maybe. I lost track." My eyes came down from the ceiling. I looked at her. Long and hard. She was draping her three-quarter checkered coat on the clothing tree and running her slender fingers around the swirling turtle-neck collar of her powder blue sweater. The matching skirt clung to her like kids hang onto their mothers. Melissa's duds always fit her like a second skin. She looked as wonderful as I remembered her.

"Well," I murmured, trying to brighten up. "And how is the winner of the Diahann Carroll Look-Alike Contest?"

"Fool," she whispered, puckering her lips at me in a kiss. "If I really looked like her, I never would have come to work for you. I wouldn't have had to. I'd be doing *Dynasty* for lots of bucks."

"Maybe so. Get all your chores done?" I was shadow-boxing, trying to find an opening. The only reassuring thing was that Mel was acting as if she had seen me that morning. As if I had never been missing, much less dead. That was something. I hung onto the notion. A drowning man ready to grab at anything familiar, all things substantial and comforting. But my hands were starting to shake.

"Uh-huh. Checks all duly deposited. Raising our Checking to two thousand and seven dollars and our Savings to a grand total of eight hundred and eighty-seven dollars and nineteen cents."

"Wow. We're thriving. How do we do it?"

"Perseverance, man. Perseverance." Her nose wrinkled. "But I couldn't find a decent card for Mike Monks. Nothing that seemed to fit. But there's still time — hey, why you fidgeting?"

I followed her concerned eyes down to my hands. Both of which were imitating adagio dancers. I laughed out loud and then put them both in my coat pockets. I made fists of them.

"Don't mind me, Mel. I'm just practicing some dance steps for the Policeman's Ball."

"Ed."

"Still here."

"You okay?" She came around the desk and put her arms around my neck. Her impossible-to-describe glims searched my face. From top to bottom. She shook her head. When she smiled, she was gorgeous. When she was serious, she was classically beautiful. "Noon, man. Don't hold out on me — we've been in the same club too long. What happened this morning at Roland's?"

Roland. Richard Roland. The name went off like a dinner gong in my skull. And all the ants and scorpions and vipers came out of hiding again. I tried not to show panic. It wasn't easy.

"Roland?" I echoed. "I don't remember —"

Melissa sniffed the air between us, sensing

now that I was being my usual cap-and-bells self. Make-Them-Laugh Ed Noon.

"Stop clowning. Are you going to take him on? You could be a big help to him in this Woody mess. You know the territory."

I unhooked Melissa's soft arms from my shoulders and spun around in the contoured chair to face the picture window. The stenos and office workers in the building across the way suddenly seemed like so many robots moving back and forth on their appointed rounds. And the air all around me was suddenly charged with high-wire tension and pure electricity.

"You think I should take his case, Mercer? Tell me what you really think, lady. I need help on this one."

"Ed, Ed. You'd be crazy not to. This is front-page stuff from here to Outer Mongolia. It could be the biggest breakthrough for you yet. Walter Woody — being forced to come out of hiding. A legend for sale. A man everybody's wondered about for years." She was talking to my back, instinctively knowing I had turned away for a reason. "If you can help Roland prove his book *is* on the level, Taft-Hartley would let you write your own ticket. No telling what your fee would be. Come on, now. Tell Mama. You saw the man — how did he strike you? Is he a con artist or what? I didn't believe the Woody character at all."

"*He's thirty-six, darkly handsome, a regular Casanova type who oddly enough is the possessor of a great writing skill. A book of his — Toward Sunset — won a prize in nineteen seventy* —" A curse from me broke that recitation up. I had been parroting Maximiliano Sacco's story to me on the jumbo jet. "Geezis —" I murmured.

"I read that book and I liked it and you have been using that word way too much lately. Ed — something's wrong. What is it? Did you throw his offer back in his face or what? Come on, now — I'm not going to stop pestering you until you tell me." I heard her heels begin to click around the desk.

"Stop," I said, quickly. In a voice I had never heard before. "Stay where you are. Don't look at me. I don't want to look at you because it will only confuse me more. Please do what I ask. There's a reason. A good, crazy reason."

There was a fast, hard silence.

I kept staring at the office workers across the way.

"All right, Ed." Her whisper was filled with love. "You going to tell me now?"

"I'm going to ask you a lot of strange questions."

"Okay."

"Weird wild questions. Nutty questions. But don't make any comments or editorialize. All I want is straight Yesses or Nos. Just bear with me. I'm begging you. I have to do it this way."

"Anything you say, Ed." Her tone was patient, kindly.

"We can do a post-mortem later, Mel. But right now I have to have some answers to a lot of things I can't explain right this minute. All I will tell you is that this is no game. No trick. No clowning around. I've never been more serious in my life."

"I told you, we've been in the same club too long — anything you do is all right with me. You know that."

"I know." I took a deep breath. "You ready for this?"

"Ready." The single word held nothing but determination and more love. I shook my head, clearing it of thoughts of her.

"Did you see me yesterday, Mel?"

"Yes."

"Where?"

"Right here."

"What was I doing."

"Nothing unusual." I thought I heard her sigh.

"Did anything out of the ordinary happen?"

"You got the phone call from Richard Roland. You talked to him a long time."

"Tell me about the phone call."

"He wanted to talk to you about helping him prove his case about Walter Woody. You made an appointment to meet him at his hotel this morning at eleven o'clock."

"The name of the hotel?"

"Essex House."

"And — I agreed to go?"

"You leaped at the chance. Things have been too quiet around here lately and you said you were on his side, that you didn't like Walter Woody types —"

"What else did I do yesterday?"

"You went to the Public Library to look up old newspaper files on Woody and Roland

and then you came back late. I closed up here and you said you wouldn't see me for dinner. That you had things to do."

"So you didn't see me again until just now?"

"That is correct. I know you when you get the bit in your teeth so I wasn't worried when I called the apartment last night. I left a message on your answering machine but you never called back —"

"And where is my apartment?"

"Huh?" That stopped even her. I guess it had to.

"The apartment. What's the address?"

There was a pause. When her answer did come, her voice was now a little funny. It had a catch in it.

"Same place it's always been. Central Park West. Number Four Fifteen — sixteenth floor."

"When you saw me yesterday what was I wearing?"

"Same clothes you have on now." She tried to raise her voice and her spirits with some humor. "You know, Ed, that Gary Cooper imitation you use on the answering machine has got to go — I mean *'Hi, Noon here —'* "

"I told you. No editorializing please. Just bear with me. I'm almost finished."

"I hope so. You're starting to worry me, now . . . ."

"Stop that. And listen to me carefully. Did I take a plane trip last year? Around September?"

"Yes."

"What for?"

"You needed a vacation. So you took two weeks off and flew to California. You said you wanted to see some old friends."

"Like who?"

"Gene Kelly, Robert Bloch, the Kemmerlings, Arte Johnson, Johnny Seven — you were going to make the rounds you said and catch up on old times — you mentioned Jane Leigh Edwards, too —

"Did I arrive safely?"

She said "Huh" again. I once found out she had an IQ of about 170 but I was giving her an awful hard time now and I knew it.

"You heard me. Did that jumbo jet, a 747, *crash*?"

"Oh, Ed, for God's sake."

"Answer the question, please."

I waited. A long time. It was that old eternity, again. I almost could hear the clock ticking on my desk. I couldn't, of course. It's an electric job but I was suspended somewhere between Life and Death. Her answer, when it came, was the one I expected, I think.

The voice behind me came on very quietly now. Soft, measured, with oceans of clarity, conviction and compassion coating every single syllable of every single word. I could hear her heart breaking.

"About six months ago, you and a couple of hundred other people crash-landed somewhere in the middle of open Wyoming. A lunatic had set off a bomb on board. But that's not important. Miraculously, the pilot set the big plane with its tail section almost gone, down safely. No one was killed. But they didn't find you right away. You and one other passenger had wandered off. Shocked, dazed. They found you hours later. You didn't have a scratch but the man with you had a knife wound in his back. Other than that, he was functioning properly. You were slightly delirious. You had to be sedated. The other man was taken to the hospital with you. But he disappeared not long after. They never found him, either —"

"Maximiliano Sacco," I said.

"Yes. That's the name you kept saying over and over again. But when they checked the passenger list, there was no one by that name on the manifest. No one else remembered him, either."

"Not even Miss Woodburn or Malvina, the stewardess."

Now, I did hear her sigh.

"Yes. We went all over that. Again and again. There was no Miss Woodburn, either. Your little old schoolteacher from Pasadena. Oh, Ed, Ed — I thought you'd gotten all this out of your system three months ago when they released you from —" She broke off, suddenly.

I still didn't turn around to look at her.

"I've been away, is that it?"

"Yes. A long rest. You needed it."

"Where?"

"Private hospital on Park Avenue. It was recommended to me. I didn't know what to do. You got great care there. A doctor named Covington took you over and straightened you out. You haven't mentioned any of this

since November when you left there. It's all
come back, hasn't it?"

"What's come back?" I asked, very carefully. I wanted to know what she knew about
me that I didn't know. "Go on. Tell me."

"Can't I look at you?" she pleaded. "It
would make it easier —"

"No," I insisted, almost like a child. "Tell
me from where you are, please, Melissa. It's
very important to me —"

"All right, Mr. Noon. Once more, you talked
about Force Five and Bardons and how this
Sacco was an android who couldn't die and
that he had wanted to hire you to do
something very bad for a million dollars —
and you also were pretty sure that Gary
Cooper wasn't dead and that not even cancer
could kill a man like him. And oh, Ed, please
turn around — I'm scared. Real scared. You
were doing beautifully until you started all
this all over again — is your head hurting
again, Ed?"

I revolved in the swivel contour chair when
I heard the tears in her voice. I looked up at
her. Saw the beautiful woman whose soul
and heart and brain were mine and something died inside me. Her lovely eyes were
brimming with tears but she was holding on
with everything she had. I couldn't go to
her — not just then.

"That bad, huh?" I shook my head and
stared down at the hands I had taken from
my pockets. But they weren't shaking anymore. They were white with repressed tension. "Sorry, Mel. Damn sorry. I knew I'd

been out to lunch but even I didn't know just
how long — guess the old hot-shot private
eye has finally flipped his lid, after all. And
after all these years . . . ."

"Oh, don't say that — don't you ever say
that to me!"

She came to me, then. Rushing. The tears
spilling, unabashed. She took me into her
arms, raining kisses all over my face. I held
onto her. Held on, hard. The room had begun
to shift on me, again, the walls tilting, the
four-drawer file dancing. I closed my eyes.
The wonderful feeling of being home again
was now gone with the wind, completely. I
was going down, for the third and very last
time. Not even a Melissa Mercer was going
to save me from drowning in my own insanity. I had joined every looney since the
beginning of Time itself. *Oh, Gary, Where
Art Thou?*

"Melissa —"

"Yes, Ed, I'm here —"

"Where's Mike? I want to see Mike Monks.
I have to talk to him — he'll listen — he
always has — get him, Melissa. Please, he
can help me out of this — please."

"Sure, Ed. Sure. See? I'm calling him right
now."

She was, too. Dialing rapidly, hardly taking her eyes off my face, looking at me
through tortured, water-filled windows. I sat
where I was. A stone man in a swivel chair. I
knew only one thing now. I had to see Mike
Monks' friendly face again. Good old Cap-

tain Michael Monks of the Homicide Department, NYPD. The only real father I ever had — he could help me, he always had.

Suddenly, the only sound in the Mouse Auditorium was the soft sobbing of Melissa Mercer.

That and a ghostly voice from somewhere in the great void, thin-lipping a quiet command:

"... *And your target is one Richard Roland. Stop him, liquidate him. The way Sacco asked you to ...*."

I heard Gary Cooper talking.

But I didn't understand anything anymore. Not even him.

Death was stronger than leaving town, all right, but taking leave of your senses must be in a class by itself.

I had never been so frightened in my life. Not ever. It was not dramatic or funny like it always is in the movies. It can never be. It hurts too much in real life. Ask the experts.

Just like alcoholics are not very amusing to the people who care for them, love them. Actors break their backs to play drunks and wackos on celluloid because they are rich, Oscar-grabbing roles but when it comes to everyday living — forget it.

Nobody loves a rummy or a mentally-ill person.

They can't. It takes too much out of them over the long haul. Alcoholism and insanity will kill love, everytime.

And my brain had left me.

My mind was an isolated, deserted, empty street where there was a weather-beaten sign that said: NO MEN AT WORK.

I felt ten years old.

13.

CLOSE ENCOUNTERS OF THE ABSURD KIND

"Mike, you know me better than any man alive."

"Sure I do."

"So you're going to have to listen to me. A long, long time. I have a lot of talking to do. A lot of things to say to you. Otherwise my head is never going to be straight again. No, Mel, don't go. You're staying, too. Turn off all the phones and lock the front door. You two know how I am. If I can talk this thing out with you — my best friend and my best girl — maybe it will all come together for me. All I know is if I don't, I'll never get back from wherever the hell I have been. Bear with me, please. You can see I'm still lucid. I can still talk a thing out. That's a good sign, isn't it? I know I'm babbling, running on, but I want to say all this, do all this, before I get cold feet, change my mind and clam up and go into a corner somewhere and not talk to anybody because maybe I couldn't bear to see the expression in their sick faces or maybe I'd be afraid they might laugh at me. You understand that, don't you? Please say you do. Let me see it in your eyes, too. I need all the help and back-up I can get."

"Sure, Ed."

Captain Michael Monks, a bachelor forever, said that in his old grim way but he never could hide the worry in his nut-brown eyes. He was also the world's worst poker player. He had never known how to bluff, either. I guess that's an art you're born with. You can't really learn it. "Go do what Ed says, Melissa. Talking this all out again just between the three of us may just be the ticket for what ails Old Motor-Mouth."

"Right, Captain. Don't go away, Ed. I'll be back in two shakes —" She blew me a kiss, her look a quick, somehow sad one. Monks shouldered to the lounge along the side wall and parked his brown topcoat and browner Borsalino. When he came back, I could see he still had the same lousy taste in ties. A thick, striped creation dangled from his burly throat. But I loved the sight of him and he had obviously dropped everything he was doing at Headquarters to answer Melissa's S.O.S. The clock on the desk now numbered 2:57. Eastern Standard Time — not nightmare hours.

Funny, but it was a good sign that I could think about his ties at a time like this. Humor can save your ass somehow.

"You need anything to drink, Ed?"

"No. I want to do this stone cold sober. How about you?"

"Good idea. Though I've known few customers who could hold their hootch as well as you do. No, thanks. I'll pass, too."

"I consider that a compliment, Captain. Coming from you."

"It is, Mr. Noon. It is."

Melissa was back in no time at all. Miss Efficient. My gift from the Yes Agency as far back as 'sixty-three. She took the seat across from me and Monks planted himself on the other office chair. They were practically flanking me, like bookends, all their attention focused in my direction. Suddenly, I was nervous all over again. Like a kid being made to recite in front of the class. A kid who didn't like to recite. Something I had never been. I had always liked to talk. Me, Sam Spade and Caspar Gutman. I shook myself loose from *that* memory and stiffened my back in the contour chair. I pyramided my ten fingers before me to keep them from break-dancing. I got hold of myself. Monks and Mel sat still. I looked at them for a long time.

They looked at me. Even longer and harder.

Nobody said anything for a few minutes. It seemed like an hour. If a mouse had walked across the auditorium, he would have been heard. If we had a mouse —

"Oh, geezis —" I stalled.

"Easy, Ed," Melissa said, softly. "Take your time. There's no rush. We're not going anywhere."

"Check," Monks growled. But I could see his eyes had never left my face. He was reading me the way he had read all his suspects for the last forty-odd years. He was one helluva cop. The best. Very little ever slipped past him when he was working.

"I feel," I said, as calmly as I could, "like a pilot taking his first solo, like a rookie coming up for his first at bat in the big leagues, like an actor giving a first reading for a part in a big Broadway show." I paused.

"Understandable," Monks grunted softly. "Considering what you've been through. Keep talking."

"It all began sometime back in August. I was in Downey's one night talking to an actor pal about Final Curtains and Death. I don't know why, but it was on my mind. I knew I was shoving off in a week or so for sunny Cal. That vacation I thought I needed so badly. I remembered saying that *Death was greater than leaving town*' and my actor pal, Bill Guhl, came back at me with one of his old lines: *Break a leg, Noon*' — that's always worth a laugh with actors but it wasn't that so much — sure, I knew I was in the mid-life crisis years, "Passages", and all that. But I had come a very long, very hard way and I had been lucky. I guess I was sort of summing up my life. No wife, no kids, not much of a bank account. Plenty of freedom, sure, but there was me and Melissa and what we had. And you, Mike — what you'd both been to me. What did I add up to but a free-wheeling selfish bum who really did his own thing and not much else? Sure, sure, I'd helped a lot of people out in my time, saved their bacon, put a lot of bad people away, but again, I was asking myself — *So What?* In the big picture, what does that all come down to, in the end? I decided — *not very much.* You might say I was one unhappy man when I kissed Melissa goodbye at Kennedy and stepped aboard that jumbo jet with little more than an attaché case and a two-suiter Tourister. I always did travel light, didn't I?"

"And you always played it alone," Monks grumbled in his old scolding way, "You damned maverick."

Somehow, the sound of him made me feel better. I pushed on.

"So that was the frame of mind I was in when Maximiliano Sacco approached my seat in the smoking section of the plane. And made his amazing offer — right out of left field."

There was no missing the way Mike Monks shifted in his chair, as if I had struck a nerve or something. I held up my hand.

"I know. There was no Maximiliano Sacco on the passenger list for Flight 717. Melissa told me. She also told me they found me walking around the desert with a little man with a knife wound in his back who later disappeared from the hospital they took us to." Ready to say more, I was checked by the sudden bright glow of happiness in Melissa Mercer's eyes.

"Ed, that's the very first time you mentioned the flight number — you remembered. That's good."

"That's right," Monks agreed, with some surprise, but his expression was puzzled, too. "We know all this, Ed. Why are you going back over the same ground?"

"To find my way. That's why. Unless I tell you what I now remember after that plane crash, you'll have no way of knowing what I've been through. Just how far over the edge I slipped. Believe me, this is Nightmare Alley with bells on. Let me finish, please."

"Sorry. Go on. I won't interrupt again."

He kept his word, too.

He and Melissa didn't say a single word until I had quietly and slowly worked my twisted path through the question-and-answer session with Dr. Charles Covington, the fantasy-visit with Gary Cooper and the Los Angeles tryst with the woman called Halina. I repeated all the dialogue I could remember including all of the Force Five-Bardon rivalry and what Richard Roland's death was supposed to mean to some nameless 'Empire'. The Helen Hamlet death at Essex House with me as the chief suspect-in-residence and possible murderer was an eyebrow-raiser that made Monks and Melissa exchange bewildered glances. So Gary Cooper was right — Covington had made all that up, very obviously. Also obviously, Mike Monks and Homicide had no such grievance on their hands. Not ever.

When I was done I was pretty damned convinced how terrible and psycho it all must have sounded but they weren't my best people for a fee. Melissa's face held nothing but sympathy and I-want-to-believe-you-Ed and Mike Monks' First Sergeant mug was knotted into pure lines and ridges of personal misery. He shook his wise owl head and his shoulders hitched again in the old Charles Bickford way.

"You know better than me how crazy that all sounds, Ed."

"Indeed I do."

"None of it is possible, all of it is improbable and what the hell can I say to you now but I-don't-know-what-to-say?"

"I know what to say. It's all finally caught up with me, the movies, the dreams, the career, the real and the unreal. I've taken a whiff into midnight and my brain is permanently damaged."

Melissa moaned, "Don't say that."

"Why not, Mel? It's true, isn't it? It may be the only true thing I've said all day."

Monks was too practical to bother with intangibles.

"According to Melissa, you called on Richard Roland today at the Essex House? Is that right?"

"She said I had an appointment but I don't remember it. I was with my Maiden From Outer Space, as far as I know."

"Hold it," Monks commanded, gruffly. "Easy enough to check that. You got the number, Melissa?"

"Yes, it's still on my appointment pad. Just a sec —"

I thought about a lot of things as she got the number for Mike and he used the desk phone to put in a call to Essex House. It didn't take long at all. Not half as long as it had taken me to find out I was riding an empty train to Nowhere. The one thing that dominated my thinking was that I had at last reached the end of my rope. After three dozen big cases, almost forty years and no counting how many tight squeezes and narrow misses, I'd run out of lives. I had certainly used up far more than nine. And I never heard a word of Mike Monks' phone palaver with Essex House. All I can remember about that now is the sudden stony silence in the office. That and coming awake, like a man out of a dream, to find them both staring at me with egg all over their faces. Monks and Melissa — the only two people on this green earth who had a claim on me.

Something was wrong.

Dead wrong.

"Well," I challenged Monks. "Did I see him or didn't I?"

"Somebody did, Ed."

"What does that mean?"

"I talked to the hotel manager. A man dressed like you and answering your general description called on Mr. Richard Roland at approximately eleven o'clock this morning. The man came down in the elevator about an hour later. You don't remember any of that at all, do you, Ed?"

"No, I don't. And why talk to the manager? Why didn't you just ask Roland if anybody named Ed Noon paid a call on him?"

Mike Monks' face was a study in helpless hard-headedness.

"Because nobody answered from Roland's

room when the desk switchboard buzzed him for me. And nobody had seen him go out again. So I got the manager to go up to his room to see if he was okay. He was not — *is* not okay — he's lying on the floor of his room with his face purple and his tongue sticking out. Somebody strangled him. The desk manager also says the room looks like a cyclone hit it. It's Murder One, Ed, and everything points to it being you, old buddy. I don't know what else to make of it. Not until Homicide shows up and looks things over. But I'm going to have to take you in, Ed. For your own good. You're not operating with a full deck for one thing. And for another, I promise you — nothing you have said to me here today will be used against you until you think it over. Do you hear me, Ed?"

"I hear you. I'm fully dressed and not in my right mind."

"Mike," Melissa wailed. "You can't — not this way — not until he has a chance to think straight, to arrange a defense."

"Stop it, Melissa," Monks growled. "You heard him same as I did. Little mystery man, plane crash he can't remember, Gary Cooper, a dame from Planet X — for Christ's sake. You think I enjoy hearing him rattle on like that? He's finally gotten dangerous. To you, to me, to everybody else. I have to take him in. For his own good."

There was no telling how far all that intramural arguing would have gone on if it wasn't for a timely interruption. Or untimely, as it turned out. The office buzzer blared and Melissa had to answer the door. When she came back, she was bearing a United Parcels package. Brown manila envelope, letter size, stuffed for mailing.

Melissa, still teary, tried to smile.

"For you, Ed. I signed for it."

"Open it," I said. Somehow, I already knew what it would contain. I think they did too. It was all in the cards all right, as certain as Death and Taxes and my sudden status as a mental incompetent. Melissa fumbled the thing open with none of her usual dexterity. It is hard to see through tears — God bless her.

Her tapering fingers emerged from the big envelope, drawing forth a stack of green crisp things that are still the finest printing job in the universe. Bills that seemed to shine even more greenly in the warm afternoon sunlight flooding the office.

"Why, they're all ten thousand dollar bills — like new — there must be at least a hundred of them!"

I laughed. A loud, brittle, humorless laugh.

A dead man's laugh.

"Sure there are," I said. "Exactly one hundred of them. Totalling one million Yankee dollars. The price Maximiliano Sacco said *they* would pay me if I liquidated Richard Roland for *them*."

"Ed," Mike Monks roared, in spite of himself. "Stop it, for God's sake — this isn't funny anymore. It's all too pat."

"It sure is," I agreed. "Lock me up, Mike. I'm a cold-blooded killer. I deserve everything that's coming to me."

That should have been the end of the whole thing.

The finale. Trail's End. The Bottom Line.

It wasn't.

Yes, I'd come to the Last Outpost, the Ultimate Climax, the Final Scene but even that wasn't meant to be. More madness was coming, further insanity was due. The Big Nuthouse's doors opened wide one more time. With another turn of the screw, and another spin of the roulette wheel.

"There's a note here," Melissa Mercer murmured, sounding dazed. "It's typed, and there's a signature —"

"Read it," I heard myself say. Monks had risen from his seat to stand alongside Melissa but his eyes were still leveled down at me like the twin barrels of a shotgun. He was still a cop, first, last and always. Homicide was his Bible — the only book he knew.

" '*Congratulations, Señor Noon . . . .* '" Melissa read aloud in an empty voice. " '*The thing is done. Bravo. We fulfill our pledges. Vaya con Dios.*' " Her face came up from the white notepaper in her trembling fingers and she too stared down at me. "It's signed *Maximiliano Sacco.*"

"Who else? Well, that's the final nail in the coffin, wouldn't you say, Captain Monks? You won't have to cuff me. I'll go very, very quietly . . . . I've had it. A Sacco letter without Vanzetti. Cute."

They say there are times in your life when you do things that have absolutely no rhyme or reason to them. No sense at all. The human condition is such that occasions will arise when one performs an act out of pure instinctive reflex. Motion, movement and coordinated motor activity which bear no relation whatsoever to any sane, cohesive train of thoughts that begin in the brain. Yet, actually, I suppose it had to start there. It has to start someplace. Even in a deranged mind, there is a light bulb going on and off.

My lights went haywire. An AC/DC scramble.

As Monks came around the desk, his expression grimmer and sadder than a cancer diagnosis, I hit him. God help me.

Even as Melissa Mercer's blues voice rose in a cry of protest and fright, I hit my best friend with everything I had. It was not a pulled punch. And it was the very first action I could remember taking in a very long time. Ages, maybe.

Monks rocketed backwards, the full force of my right fist catching him dead-center on the point of his chin. His head flew back with an awesome crack and then he was out of sight. Melissa rushed me, hands outstretched, half-imploring, half-retaliating. I could no longer tell which. I did not hit her. But I did something just as bad. I straightarmed her out of my path, slamming her across the torso, just above the breasts. She literally sailed out of my way, going down in a disorganized sprawl in the direction of the picture window. I was pure animal just then. All fear, totally involved in only one thing. Wanting to get out, to escape, to find some safe hole in the earth where I could lick my wounds and think only of my own hide. Self-preservation, the most basic and thoroughly selfish emotion of them all, had me by the balls.

I barreled for the outer office, the front door, the elevators, not looking back. And worst of all, not caring whether I had killed Monks, hurt Melissa or left a million dollars in nice green bills all over the floor of the auditorium. I didn't even know if I was wearing my licensed .45 calibre Colt automatic. I was gone, man. Really gone. Completely off my nut.

There was a crowd in the tiled corridor.

A mob, really.

I saw Gary Cooper and Dr. Charles Covington. Halina was smiling her stainless steel smile from the depths of the elevator car whose doors were sliding open. Little Maximiliano Sacco, white suit, no moustache and all, was chatting amiably with Miss Woodburn and Malvina, the airline flight hostess.

Gary Cooper's lean, haunting face wore the saddest smile I had ever remembered. He had his hands poked into the side pockets of the O'Hara trenchcoat and he was wearing the flying helmet and goggles this time. Not the slick snappy fedora that always looked as if it had been made just for him.

There was a hum of sound in the atmosphere. A mighty noise, a concentrated drone. As if some gigantic spacecraft was hovering just above us all. I looked up, bewildered, half-expecting to see a gleaming, iridescent, mind-boggling spectacle. Sacco, the women and the Ace did not look up at all. Halina was emerging from the elevator car, glittering nakedly again, her hair dazzling, radiant. Her teeth were fangs, now.

Dr. Covington was looking at his watch, as if he had an urgent appointment someplace. His head was bandaged, blood-stained.

There was nothing above me but limitless blue space.

With a million twinkling stars.

A comet flashed, trailing fiery sparks, disintegrating in a burst of red glare. An asteroid came hurtling by. Some far-off planet glowed in the endless distance. I have never known one from the other — I can only recognize Saturn. This was not Saturn.

I never did reach all the familiar faces in the corridor.

Something got between us.

A swirling, curling, twisting, monstrous apparition that kept changing shape, elongating, contracting, expanding and yet all the while snarling and hissing at me. Clouds of steam filled the distance dividing us. My very own Nyarlothotep, my private Crawling Chaos. I screamed, and then screamed again. I struck out wildly. Slashing, flailing. My arms felt like ten-ton snakes.

"... *It's a hard year and a dark night,*" I heard Gary O'Hara Cooper say and I almost smiled.

I also heard General Yang's voice suddenly, rendered in that heavy Russian accent of Akim Tamiroff's that was so individual.

"No humming bird can fight fifteen wolves, Mr. O'Hara."

The Id Monster closed in on me, swarming, engulfing, spreading out until it filled the whole corridor, the entire world, the total universe of the mind. Golden globes rotated, pinwheels coruscated, multi-colored streamers unfurled, missiles thundered, spaceships blasted off their gantries. Galaxies opened up, the limitless blue of Up There beckoned. I was trapped in a kaleidoscope, looking out. I left this planet Earth —

Going where no man had ever dared go before.

Or ever could.

To the Undiscovered Country.

The territory of the Mind. The Forbidden Planet.

Shakespeare was right again, as usual.

So was Hollywood.

14.

TALL BLUE SHADOWS
BEHIND US

There the Milky Way, there Orion, there the North Star riding at a hard right angle from the top of the pot that formed the Big Dipper .... I saw them all as I shot into space. They might have been the RCA Building, the Statue of Liberty, the World Trade Center or the George Washington Bridge, all lit up and sparkling brilliantly on a frosty winter night. But they weren't. They were what they were and I saw them because I was flashing among them. Weightless, airless, breaking any existing speed records for mere mortals. Superman was a piker compared to me. I could fly, too. And it didn't seem to be cause for alarm or wonder or even satisfaction. It was simple fact.

Dark blue impenetrable sky loomed.

Impassive, cold, inexorably vast and impossible.

I might have been a shooting star, lost in space.

There was no sound at all, not so much as a whisper. The Big Vacuum had me. I was outward bound. Heading only for more space, more endless blueness, the extra-dimensional void. I wasn't sure of anything. All I was aware of was a heady sensation of Buck Rogers-Flash Gordon-Man Of Steel power. Mightier than a few dollars worth of minerals and chemicals and ninety one percent water. I was great. I was It. Somebody up there liked me — I had the universe by the tail. Einstein, Fermi, Von Braun, Teller, Oppenheimer — rookies of the drawing board. I was doing what they had never left their desks and labs for. The orbit, the force field, the Galactic blueprints, were all mine alone. I had conquered Space.

No pressurized suit, no globular helmet, no air line, no equipment, no nothing. I was doing it all.

The blinding stars glittered, the deep blue sky got bluer, the vast wasteland went on forever. On a clear day I could have seen Everything. On this dark night, I saw just as much.

My earthly problems, the mental turmoil, the steady nightmare, had dissolved into nothingness. I didn't remember a thing. It was Nirvana, yesterday's gardenias, old news.

And then I started to fall.

The dizzying headlong propulsion was checked. As if I had come up against an invisible stone wall. There was no violence, no pain, no sharp Stop Motion effect.

I only stopped moving forward.

And dropped downward. Like a plumb bob.

Falling. Breaking every aerodynamic rule on the books.

The stars went out, the blue sky vanished, the mass objects all around me faded to black. Blacker, blackest . . . ebony . . . .

"Zavoda, the Noseless One, awaits you, *Eduard Mittag.*"

"Who me?"

"Yes, Earthman. He has awaited you for a great length of time. A hundred of your light years."

"Well, I don't know him and I don't know you. And why not call me Earthling like they do in all the comic books and serials?"

"We have outgrown such ancient usage. You are a man of the planet Earth. We of Bardo have decided to rule you the way you should be ruled. Know only that you are honored that Zavoda considers an audience with you."

"I'm thrilled. It makes my peepee real hard. And who the hell are you? I can't see you. You're nothing but a shadow and a voice out of thin air."

"I am Harachai, Blood-Guard to the Lord Zavoda. And your eyes have not the power to see a Bardon. It is no more complex than that. But come — *Eduard Mittag* — the time is at hand."

"My German is a mite rusty but *Eduard Mittag* is Ed Noon — why do Bardons use the language of the Teutons? Don't tell me the Fourth Reich made Outer Space after all these years?"

"Silence. All will be explained to you soon enough. Follow me and say no more until Zavoda speaks."

In this most cosmic of all my nightmares and dreams, the free flight had terminated somehow and I was now walking in a pink and purple wonderland of corridors and hallways. Gigantic ones which dwarfed me to a dot. The shadow before me was tall and deep blue. And about six more trailed behind me. Shadows, nothing but shadows. But I could see they were solid. I didn't feel as if I could poke my fist through one of them. I didn't try. The high, reedy voice which had welcomed me to Bardo, wherever the hell that was, didn't sound like someone you could play games with. Especially rough stuff.

Besides, I was the stranger in the strange land. That old classic condition. When you're one of those, it is best to do nothing until someone asks you to. So I followed after the tall blue shadow, wondering all the while where my sanity had gone.

I looked down at myself. Mercifully, the Brooks Brothers suit, the black *Roma* shoes, the blue foulard tie. I'd half expected nakedness or warrior robes or a suit of mail or an outfit worn in the service of the Emperor Ming. The way things had been going lately for me, Murphy's Law was working overtime. Darwin, Newton and Mendel weren't doing too well either.

"Anything that can go wrong will go wrong," I said, out loud, to no one in particular, least of all Harachai's tall, blue, advancing figure up front. Tacking on the corollary, *". . . And if anything does go wrong, it will happen at the most inopportune time. So help me, Orlando J. Murphy."*

"Silence!" The Harachai shadow commanded. *"Speak no more."*

I spoke no more. I dogged the tall shadow's heels. If he had heels. Behind me, the squad of also-blue shadows trailed.

The mammoth corridors and hallways suddenly narrowed, trimming down to a long, tunnel-like world. Harachai's shadowy head seemed almost to touch the dull purplish ceiling. There was no sound, no noise at all. My own size tens touching the floor beneath them might have been phantom gliders. There were no bad memories running around in my brain. No good ones, either. I had achieved some kind of state of grace. Knowing only my identity and hardly anything else. No Past, no Present, not much concern about the Future, either. Joe Cool on parade, who thought nothing of meeting shadows from other worlds. All in a day's work — a piece of cake, as easy as rolling off a log or closing your fingers around a nice, fat retainer.

A row of lights winked up ahead. The tunnel ended. The tall blue shadow before me disappeared. Just like that. So did the crew of blues behind me. I tried to blink my eyes. I couldn't. They synchronized badly. They wouldn't shut. The winking lights began to rotate endlessly. Also, I found I could not move forward. I had body English but it did not extend further than my nose. There might have been an invisible glass wall built all about me. My periphery of physical motion was all of a foot to all points of the compass. I did not panic. The winking lights extinguished. The pinkly-purplish world evaporated. Now it was kind of a North Pole wasteland. Glittering carpets of deathly white ice stretching into Infinity. I waited. There was nothing else to do. It was somebody's else's party. Or ballgame. I was only a visiting player. If I was to play at all.

"Okay, Zavoda," I called. "Come out, come out, wherever you are."

To my own ears, it was the barest whisper.

The ice-like, polar aspect of this new world suggested winds and Arctic chill but there was none of that. Zilch.

Only a timeless, non-feeling *nothingness* . . . .

"Eduard Mittag . . ." The two words, the name, abruptly came forth from somewhere in a voice that sounded like it needed Three-In-One oil. A disembodied voice. I saw nothing at all around me but the Admiral Byrd landscape. The voice might have come from any direction.

"Here. And I wish I wasn't."

"But you are here and here you will stay."

"For how long?"

"Long enough." There was a pause. "I am Zavoda the Noseless One."

"I figured that out already. Harachai, your butler, showed me in. Remember?"

"It is true, then. What the Bioliner told us about you."

"Bioliner —"

"Yes. A device that records all data and history and events about you. The Personality check underscored your idiosyncratic mode of speech, your habitual tendency to mouth inane, non-humorous remarks when faced with great danger."

I shrugged — a tight shrug, considering my walled-in sense of restriction. "Am I in great danger, O Noseless One?"

"Danger is a primitive state. There is no reason inherent in the condition. Yet a set of circumstances can exist which would place even an earthman such as yourself in a state of that which you choose to term *danger*."

"That's double-talk and you know it. And call me a mindless primitive. But please tell me — what the hell is all this? And what is the score?"

"Score? Of course. A sports term signifying total of points tallied. Archaic, really. Still, I will converse with you on your own terms and in your native idiom. Perhaps, it will simplify our discourse."

"Discourse away, Zavoda." I couldn't resist jibing that faceless voice. What did it matter whether it was noseless or not? Nothing made much sense, anyway. "I haven't the foggiest."

It was as if I was standing up straight in the middle of some vast Nowhere, talking to the wind, the earth, the sky. But of course there were none of those things. Just me and lost horizons, the other side of the moon and simon-pure Wasteland. Not so simple, at all. This outer space Fortress Of Solitude was a doozy.

"Eduard Mittag —"

"Still here. And still wishing I wasn't."

"Be patient. I shall explain to you what has happened to you. The Time Warp seems to have disoriented you. The Hasslein Curve, that bend in Time, named for your Earth-Scientist who discovered it — has brought you here. You fell through the Cosmos. A microcosm in the macrocosm. Bardo became your, shall we say, destination? Harachai and the Blue Shadows found you entering our magnetic field. And yet — and yet —" The tinny, oil-can voice almost seemed to chuckle. "You were scheduled for this journey, this time, this moment with me, a long long millennium ago. In your Earth idiom — *it was written in the stars.*"

"Which you're saying I fell from. Okay. Go on. There must be more. Or this is the LSD trip to end all LSD trips."

Again, the slightest of pauses.

"I do not know that letter-classification. But no matter. During your stay on earth, one day, you boarded an aircraft. You were on your way to a place called California, a state of a union of contiguous territories known as the United States. Measured in units of your earth calendar, it was the year One-Nine-Eight-Seven. During the flight of this aircraft from a place known as New

York, you met an individual who called himself Maximiliano Sacco." The voice halted. "Do you remember any of what I am telling you?"

"No. But don't let that stop you. Keep talking."

"I shall. Maximiliano Sacco, knowing of your occupational skills as a private investigator, offered you a fee of one million dollars in your American currency, to liquidate a man called Richard Roland. A man who was a threat to Sacco and his, shall we say, colleagues?"

"Say anything you like, Zavoda. I haven't a clue yet as to what this is all about."

"Have no fear. Memory will return even as I speak and add more detail. An after-effect of Time Warp travel is a temporary shutdown of the Memory Banks. But let me continue — before you could accept Sacco's proposal, and money, there was a disaster on board the air vehicle. An explosive device was set-off by a passenger intent on his own destruction. The Seven-Four-Seven — such was its identifying designation, made a crash landing in the deserts of a state named Wyoming. A miraculous feat of flying ability saved the plane and the lives of all on board. All were saved. Including the earth man who is yourself and the Replicon who was Maximiliano Sacco. Sacco who was from this very planet. One of the finest Bardons of us all. Our Special Emissary from this cosmos, sent to contact you."

Something stirred in my skull. But the light wouldn't go on. Not just yet. I put my hands in the pockets of my nice Brooks Brothers suit. I got a shock. My right hand closed over the cold but reassuring butt of a Colt .45. My own little equalizer. There was no mistake, either. I'd have known that gun anywhere. Funny, I hadn't been conscious of its weight at all. And why wasn't it in my shoulder holster which was the only bed it had ever known?

"More," I begged. "I need more."

"Yes. Of course." Zavoda's metallic voice clicked. "Unfortunately, the aircraft catastrophe, such as it was, demoralized you. You suffered what is called on your planet a nervous breakdown. You were committed to the care of one experienced in such matters. A mental disorder expert, a pychiatrist, designated Doctor Charles Covington. Equally unfortunately, Covington was one of the most efficient officers of Bardo's traditional enemies — *Force Five*. The English definition for a planet whose title is a name you would find impossible to pronounce. No Bardon has ever been able to say the name clearly. Therefore, we refer to it always as *Force Five*."

The tiny light was beginning to flicker.

Faintly. But it was flickering.

"I'm still listening, Zavoda."

"Yes, you are, are you not? The Replicon Covington tried to seduce you, twist your mind yet further. He very nearly succeeded in his attempt to divert you from the assassination, if you will, of Richard Roland, the name which Force Five had built into a legend to further their scheme to take over the planet Earth."

The light went on. It did not flicker anymore but burned steadily. A regular Thomas Edison electric light — a bulb like that first one in Menlo Park. A million dollar firefly.

"I hit him with a chair — I ran away —"

"Yes. And then we sent you our emissary Halina."

"The stainless steel playmate —"

"And you co-ordinated with her on a grand scale. Until you were at last free. Free to return to your former world — your office — the affair listed on your Bioliner as *The Mouse Auditorium* —"

"And you sent me Gary Cooper too — what about him?"

There was but one more of those metallic halts.

"No," Zavoda said, very clearly and very firmly. "We did not send you Gary Cooper. We knew of him, certainly, and of his influence upon your mind and lifestyle. The thought occurred to us that you would listen to him no matter what state of mind you were in. Yet, oddly enough, we found him impossible to replicate. The model resisted all our best efforts. In the end, we had to surrender the plan. It was as if the mold had been broken when he was created. No, we did not send you Gary Cooper. If you saw him, then he was a product of your own vivid yet complex imagination, *Eduard Mittag*."

"Call me Ed Noon," I snapped. It was a marvel, all right. "Then you really didn't send me Cooper? I conjured him up, because I needed him, because I wanted to see him again. He knew I'd believe what he told me. But God Almighty, I saw him so plain. I could touch him. Why, he even decked me —"

"Decked? I do not understand."

"Sorry. I mean he hit me. Right smack on the button. A humdinger of a punch. Like old times. Like old movies. Like —"

"Like Life itself?"

"Like Life itself," I agreed, feeling warm all over. Then I shook myself. "You know all the rest, then — what happened when I finally did get back to my office?"

"*Before* you went back to your office, my friend." Zavoda's voice was almost maddeningly subtle.

"What do you mean, *before*?"

"You went to Essex House and you liquidated Richard Roland as you wanted to do. As Maximiliano Sacco had hired you to do. Why do you think we sent you one million dollars?"

"That's crazy," I said. "I'd never kill anybody for money. I couldn't. I don't even remember Richard Roland. I wouldn't have known what he looked like. You're lying, you're trying to trick me for some nutty reason —"

Zavoda's voice made its almost-laughing sound again.

"You still don't understand, do you, Ed Noon? The Time Warp. This moment you now spend with me is over one thousand years later. From the moment you struck the two people who meant more to you than anyone else on that planet Earth which you loved so much — to this pin-point of *Now* — *you came here*. It is all done. We of Bardo rule your Earth planet from our position in the galaxy. There is no more Earth as you knew it. All those people, those places, those things you knew so well, are all gone. Gone with the limitless, endless particles of the past — you are now in the Year Two Nine Eight Nine, as you once calculated time. Look around you. This is the Universe of the Present. Yours of the Past terminated long, long ago. There is no more planet Earth, Earthman."

"You're not telling me the truth — you're making this all up to confuse me, the way Sacco did. God, he was knifed! The bomber on the plane —"

"Yes. A temporary break-down of Sacco's systems. He misinterpreted the attack. He thought it was an agent of Force Five attempting to thwart his mission with you —"

"I don't believe you!" I shouted, in spite of myself. "This is all screwy — a trick — a plot. You're doing what Covington did. And Halina, too — and Mike Monks and Melissa, God help them. You all planned this — to drive me up the wall and around the bend."

"I must caution you against hysteria. It will serve you nothing but remorse and further disorientation."

"Up yours, Zavoda! Way way up —"

My fingers closed tightly about the .45 Colt.

The hollow voice droned on:

"It is useless to deny a fact simply because your mind will not accept what your eyes cannot see and your ears cannot hear."

"I can't see you and I don't want to hear you either, Zavoda, and I'm through with all this madness — this cock-eyed, mind-bending loop-de-loop you've all put me on. Through, do you hear me, Noseless One — *through!*"

On the word, the .45 cleared my pocket.

Invisible Zavoda did laugh, then.

A tin-man's laugh. If you could call it that. Him, that.

I raised the automatic and fired, never taking my finger off the trigger. I gave him the whole clip, whether I could see him or not. Blasting toward the direction of the voice, somewhere up there ahead of me, until the hot hammer clicked on an empty chamber.

And then the damn thing blew up in my hand.

With all the thunder and violence of a little Hiroshima.

The explosion, when it came, rocketed me to Eternity.

And back among the stars. And the black hole of Nowhere. Out There.

Zavoda, like the Empire, had struck back.

I was in Warp Drive again.

15.

E.T. AND T.S.

She crouched, draped above me, those splendid mammaries still suspended close by. Her exploding golden hair hung about her oval face like a mushroom cloud. There was no escape, no matter what she was saying. I was hooked into Movieland and my own madness as surely as there were five Dionne Quintuplets, Seven Lively Arts, and Six Black Horses for every old funeral in the West of long ago ....

"Halina ... You again ... ?"

"Yes, Edward. I am here because of your need."

"Oh, God, Halina. Getting laid isn't going to solve any of this mess for me. It didn't before. Only made things worse."

"You still do not understand, foolish Edward. Living in the past. Those archaic, obsolete frames of reference ...."

"What the hell are you talking about now?"

"You know very well what I mean. I can read the telescreen of your thought processes. Dionne Quintuplets, Seven Lively Arts and Six Black Horses. You are sadly out of date with your times, Edward Noon. Why not rather *The Cosby Show, Family Ties* and *L.A. Law?* Those landmarks of the period of the Thirties have become all too ancient, Edward."

"Stop it! Stop it! Don't read my mind — how did I get back to you?"

"Don't you know?"

"How could I know? I, who am out of my skull?"

"Zavoda sent you back to me. You were not yet ready for life on Bardo. Your graph still shows irregularities. The residue of your former days. Until that is cleansed from your soul, purged from your memory, you must go back to your own time. And your own planet. Surely, you can comprehend such a thing. On Bardo, there must be only Bardo. It is the *credo* of all Bardons. They live by that."

"Of course. What the hell else?"

"You are unhappy once more, Edward."

"Who me?"

"Yes. There are lines of misery and suffering in your face. Come, let Halina give you succor."

"Sure, why not? Succor me all you like. . . ."

She did. As she had before.

On the big wide bed with the picture window and the great view of downtown Los

Angeles. No, that wasn't right. You can't see the canyons and hills and the twinkling lights from anywhere but the high ground. What a laugh. I had never been higher in my life. And the roller-coaster ride to Oblivion was still going on. Between two worlds, lost in space, twenty thousand leagues under the sea — from here to eternity — to hell and back — the sky above and the mud below — all the titles and phrases fit. But what did they fit and where would it all end?

I didn't know. Halina didn't either.

For all her spooky, esoteric talk.

She merely did me again, in her piston-like, relentlessly methodical way. Draining me with all of her hungry orifices and whatever and whoever willed her to do just that.

"There. You will feel better soon. The lines have departed from your face. Your eyes are restful now."

"Are you a Replicon too, Halina? An android gizmo?"

"I am Halina."

She was poised once more at the foot of the bed, her too-perfect figure curled as she rested on her knees. The golden explosion of hair framed her oval, chiseled face. The weird eyes gleamed in the gloom of the room, unblinkingly. I had the feeling that if I dropped a quarter in her navel she would start screwing me all over again. I had surrendered to the whole fantasy-cockamamie-nightmare-dream-nutville thing now. There was no more fight left in me. I was also sure I was in my own private Hell. The sort of strange world where I was being strung out and tortured for all the wildly improbable, impossible dreams I had dreamed all my living days. If Gary Cooper showed up one more time, I was going to ask him — no, beg him — to take me with him. To Cloud Nine or Valhalla or that Big Movie House In The Sky. It was Over and Out, as far as I was concerned. Or cared.

I waited for Halina to evanesce, to shimmer, and dissolve, and fade away like last time. But she had not moved from her classic posture at the foot of the bed. A Bhudda with a body.

"You want me to go now, Edward."

"You read my mind."

"Yes. Yet I also sense something else."

"Such as?"

"You are not wishing to go back to your office this time. Your Mouse Auditorium."

"You got it, Halina."

"Why not, may I ask?"

"What good would it do? I don't know where I'm at or which end is up. I'm not going back there to ask a lot of silly questions I don't have the answers for. Nor can I account for any of the actions people will tell me I did. I'm tired . . . Halina. More tired than I have ever known . . . all I want to do is sleep for a thousand years . . . and I don't care much when or where I wake up."

"Poor Edward."

"You can say that again."

"Poor Edward."

I laughed even if my soul was in the bottom of my shoes.

"You damned assembly-line company

whore — buzz off. All my biological devices are satisfied. You did your standard good job. Thank you and goodbye. See you around."

"I'm glad to have pleased you once more, Edward."

"And I'm glad that you're glad. So long, Halina."

"Farewell, Edward."

I closed my eyes, not wanting to see the magical disappearing act again. I didn't. But I heard it all the same. A hissing and whistling kind of sound, accompanied by a flash of strange heat. And then she was really gone. It was as if the room had never known her. The bed was still made and I was fully clothed. I was even wearing my pork-pie hat in bed, pulled down tightly over my brow. Wow. I'm telling you. I was in great shape. Real great shape. The rubber room hadn't been built that could hold the likes of me.

And there was more to come.

Much, much more. And then some.

There is no limit to the sky when you're off your rocker.

Time Travel had become standard operating procedure for me.

You might say, a way of life.

A cluster of fleecy clouds was the next thing I saw. I was walking along their soft, absorbent cotton whiteness as nice as you please. There was no sunlight but it was a gorgeous, heavenly day all the same. The cloud banks were at my knee-level and they parted eerily and silently as I pushed through them. I seemed to be all alone on a sea of *cumulus* laid out in pleasant lanes of tufty snow. Ed Morris, the only pilot I had ever known, used to tell me how much he loved nosing a jet through them for they signalled nothing but fine flying weather. I knew what he meant now. I felt euphoric. Like walking on air. Nothing was on my mind.

I saw him then.

The Ace.

The One-Of-A-Kind Man.

Frank James Cooper, born in Helena, Montana, graduate of Grinnell College, would-be-cartoonist, one-time cowboy extra and then the ultimate leading man in movies. Christened Gary by a grateful Hollywood, California, who showed him off to the world. A star of the first magnitude. The real thing.

He was leaning against a shadowy hitching post rolling a cigarette. He wasn't dressed like O'Hara anymore. No. It was the ten gallon hat, the neckerchief, the buttoned-down shirt and the chaps of *The Virginian*. That surprised me a little. He looked so much younger. But he was as bronzed, as elegantly lanky and as handsome as ever. I could have picked him out of a thousand range riders.

"It was as if the mold had been broken when he was created." Zavoda had said it all.

When I reached him, he barely glanced up from the makings between his long, spatulate fingers. But I knew he knew I was there. The vibes were right.

"Howdy, Ed," he murmured, as if he had seen me that morning for breakfast. The clipped greeting said so much more than two little words.

"Tell me the truth, Coop." I tried to keep my tone as light as possible. I knew how he hated maudlin messages.

"Meaning?"

"I've bought the farm, haven't I? Just like you did twenty-seven years ago."

He finished rolling the cigarette. He popped the white cylinder into his mouth and dug out a match from the breast pocket of the shirt. His cornflower blue eyes regarded me coolly for a moment before he said. "Is that what you think?" Then he thumbed the match into flame and I marveled again at the sleekness of his every move and gesture. Never a wasted motion, nary an excessive action. He must have invented the technique actors always called *Underplaying*.

"That's what I think. It's the only thing I can think. I've gone too far in too little time. I left a mess downstairs that I don't understand, much less remember. I've been places and done things that can't be done by ordinary people. Not anyone that's *alive*, anyway. And I even dreamed you up when I wanted to. And here you are again. Isn't that proof enough?"

"Maybe. Maybe not."

"Come on, Coop. Don't be laconic with me now. Not at this late date. If it's over for me, I want to know. I have a right to know. I never believed in Heaven or Hell as geographical locations, like Manhattan and Brooklyn, but — please. Tell me."

He exhaled two streams of blue smoke

from his famous nostrils and then regarded the tip of the burning cigarette. As if the answer was there someplace.

"So you think you're dead, huh?"

"D.O.A. all the way from where I'm standing."

"Did you figure out how you died, Ed?"

"The plane. It crashed when the bomb blew some of it away. I never could have gotten out alive. Neither could anybody else. Including Sacco, whatever the hell he really was. That's what I think. All the rest of this weird brain-ride I've been on is merely wishful thinking. Me wanting to live. The private detective still wanting to work on a case. I always had a death wish, you know. It was a gag I always used —"

"And what might that be, Ed?"

"I want to live!"

His smile was Memory Lane again. I'd seen that smile thousands of times. "That's right clever, Ed. Just like you too. But, you see, it's like this — you thinking you're dead isn't really where it's all at. Or what it's all about, either."

"I need more than that. Lots more."

"Sure you do and I reckon an explanation is coming to you. Only thing is, I'm not the one to do it."

"Come again?"

He put the cigarette to his lips, held it there as he puffed, his eyes thoughtful. He shook his head, slowly.

"No, Ed. I can't do it. This range isn't my property. You might say I'm just a saddle bum here. Riding through. You'll have to talk to the head man."

"And who the hell is that?" I almost snapped at him because I was so confused and unhappy again. "St. Peter? Cecil B. De Mille? God — ?"

Gary Cooper straightened up. The cigarette was forgotten.

The blue eyes no longer looked friendly.

They were leveled, icy, grim.

"You got no call talking like that, Ed. Not you. Not the kind of man you've been."

"All right —" I softened, calming down. "But you don't have to tell me. I think I already know. I'm dead. And I hope Benny Marinelli is up here, that sweetheart of a bartender. And Bill Daprato — a guy I have to thank for a million laughs — I've missed them both for years — and Alma — and I don't know how I rated Heaven but this must be the place if you're here, Coop. Okay. I'm convinced now. I'm ready —"

"This isn't Heaven, Ed," Gary Cooper said quietly with that make-no-mistake quality. The voice before the shoot-out at high noon.

"Then what, the clouds, the sunshine, the peace and quiet —"

"It's a way station. A Between-Place. And you have to go back, Ed. Down there where you came from. That's the whole thing."

I blinked. "What are you saying?"

"I'm saying it's not over yet. Your job isn't finished. You still got to get to it. And right quick. There's still time enough to straighten the whole rodeo out."

There was no quarreling with him. Not the way he was looking at me now. The lips were set tight, the jaw was firm, the eyes sadly regretful — and wise.

I shook myself. "But how do I get back? Just wish myself there or go on another of those mind-bending flights of fantasy I've been on? I can't. I'm worn out. I'm beat."

"I'll do it for you, Ed. I owe you that much."

"You? How —"

He hit me again, Gary Cooper did. Another one of those right-from-the-shoulder beauties that travels in a short, straight line. Whoever gets on the other end of one of those smashers has to go down. And Out.

I did.

The universe of clouds, sun, peacefulness, and Gary Cooper, vanished in one revolution of sight, sound and senses. The mad tea party was far from over. Very far.

I dropped through the hole in the sky.

A ceiling came into focus somewhere. There was a fly walking along it, taking all the time in the world.

Then I saw a chair.

Then a bed.

Then a face.

The face above me loomed moon-like with green eyes that glared. I know a cop when I see one. This was a cop. They all wear their fedoras that way, as if they were mad at their hats. Pulling them down tight over their foreheads.

"'Bout time you woke up. C'mon. Get yourself together. You got a lot of explaining to do, Noon."

Strangely, I was calm. Lying on my back with a plainclothes man crowding me, spouting the same old lines I'd heard all my life, in a million movies. They never changed, those lines.

"What did I do now?" I asked, my voice sounding like it came from a planet far, far away. "I just got here."

The moon face, just as round and smooth, except for the fuming green eyes, tried not to laugh at me. But the wide mouth pulled back in a pure grimace of disgust and contempt.

"You're gonna say you don't remember a thing, is that it?"

"That's it. I don't remember a thing."

"Sure you don't. They never do. On your feet, shamus. I'll give you a good look at what you did."

He didn't let me get up by myself, he yanked me up, and none too gently. I came to a standing position, rocking, swaying. He stepped back, a man as tall as myself, but burlier, meaner. I tried to collect what little was left of my senses. I had just left Gary Cooper or, rather he had dropped me. With a sucker punch, out of some heavenly wasteland, back down to Earth again. *And what, exactly?*

"I'm O'Connor. Detective Sergeant Poe O'Connor. NYPD. I'll read your rights to you before I haul your tail out of here. Just remember I told you, huh? You have the right to remain silent until you get a lawyer to fight for your rights — and don't try to get cute later on and say I didn't tell you and we'll get along fine. C'mon. Stop blinking your eyes like you don't know which end is up. I'm wise to you. Look at that —" He wasn't asking. He grabbed my arm and jerked little old me to the left so that I was facing the side of the hotel room. For a hotel room it had to be. A fancy one. The kind that no fly had any right to be in. The furnishings, the upholstery, the window with the drapes were all First Class Manhattan. It had to be Manhattan. I got a flash of wide-open, yawning Central Park through the huge window. The trees never looked greener.

"Essex House — right?" I heard myself say.

"Sure, Noon. But what about *that*, huh?"

That was a corpse. A female one.

Someone who had been extremely shapely, very, very tall, with dark hair. Almost jet black. I saw Sasson jeans, a three-quarter toggle coat. Scotch plaid design. Three-inch spikes jutted from her stiffened feet. She was lying on her side, her face twisted away from me. Something ticked in my head. Like an insistent clock that had to be heard, that would be heard, no matter what. An alarm clock.

"Well, Noon, I'm waiting. Talk."

"Is she wearing a Star of David and a gold crucifix around her neck?"

"She is."

"Is her name Helen Hamlet?"

"It is."

"Then something's wrong here. Real wrong."

I wasn't looking at him. I was looking at her. And all around the room. For things I could not find because they weren't there.

"Okay. You admit knowing her." Detective Sergeant O'Connor's tough voice blasted my right ear. "Now say a lot more. Like why you killed her — couldn't have been for a piece of ass."

"She's not dead," I said. "She can't be."

"No? You want to check her pulse? She's getting cold already. I make book you put the blocks to her over two hours ago —"

"You don't understand, O'Connor. This isn't right. The whole set-up is wrong. It wasn't the way — it *isn't* the way it's supposed to be, if it happened at all."

"You're not making sense. But help yourself. Keep talking until my partner gets here. I'm going to need a hand with you. What don't I understand, Noon?"

"For one thing, she's not supposed to die until she goes into convulsions at the hospital they take her to. Roosevelt Hospital, it was. And she's dressed now. She's supposed to be naked. Me too. and why isn't the room on fire? It was supposed to be burning brightly according to the next-door room guests who sounded the alarm — right?"

"The Dills," O'Connor grunted, in a strange, faraway voice. "Basil and Rosemary. English — real tourists."

"You see? I knew that, didn't I? How

could I know that? And why is Helen
Hamlet wearing all her clothes and how did I
kill her by the way, just for the record, and
where are all the bottles? We were hootch-
ing it up, weren't we? That's what Dr.
Covington told me, didn't he? He said we
had both been drinking — '*something incredible*' "

"Easy, cowboy. Slow down. You're getting
hysterical."

"Answer my questions. I just remembered
something else. Her clutch bag. Where's her
clutch bag with that stuff in it that was in
the drinks that made her pass out —"

Detective Sergeant Poe O'Connor came
around me and blocked my view of crumpled
Helen Hamlet. He did not put his hands on
my shoulders to steady me, though I could
see he wanted to. No. His hand was buried in
the side pocket of his overcoat. Probably
wrapped around his service revolver. I
couldn't exactly blame him. I had worried
him. Worried him plenty. The last thing a
cop wants is to be alone in a hotel room with
a psycho while he waits for his partner and
more cops to show up. That doesn't make
their day.

"Go sit down in that chair over there,
Noon. Where I can see you. And stop babbling. You're talking crazy, man."

"Am I?" I smiled. "No crazier than a name
like Poe O'Connor. What kind of a name is
that?"

He almost grinned, in spite of what his experienced police mind was telling him about
me and my condition. "Irish. My old lady

was an Edgar Allan Poe nut. Used to read him aloud to me when I was a runt. Never understood them much but they used to scare the hell out of me. Especially that one about the black cat —"

"Sure they would." But my mind was already somewhere else, like it had been so very much lately. "The Dills. Basil and Rosemary. Geezis. Those are the names of three spices —"

"Three spices," O'Connor echoed stupidly.

"Yeah. Spices. Like sugar, salt, thyme, cinnamon —"

"Take it easy, Noon. And sit down like I asked you to."

I didn't sit down. My smile got wider, sillier, loonier."

"Yeah. Crazy, isn't it? Like your name's crazy and their names are crazy and this whole set-up is crazy — crazy, crazy, crazy."

"Noon, I'm warning you —"

"And I'm warning you, O'Connor. I'm as crazy as a bedbug and the whole universe is crazier still and there's only one thing left for me to do before I take up permanent residence in the psychiatric ward at Bellevue. Know what that is?"

He couldn't help himself. He asked, "What?" as his awed and frightened eyes tried to read my face — and my meaning. He was too late to do anything about them. Later than late.

Maybe the black cat scared him as a kid but I gave him a descent into the maelstrom and a premature burial.

I zapped him with my ray gun.

And he fell like the House of Usher.

Even as he toppled, I had run past him, heading for the front door. There was no sense in looking back. How could I trust anything I saw or heard now, with the condition I was in? I never did ask myself where the ray gun had come from. All of a sudden, it was just there.

I know they don't call them ray guns anymore — not since the old Buck Rogers days but that didn't matter.

Nothing much did.

I had gone as far as insanity could take me. There was nothing else to do but die.

Properly. Decently. Normally.

Without all the fuss, the feathers, the confusion, the sheer Coney Island Fun House madness of it all.

Help me, anybody.

16.

YOU CAN'T BEAT THE MACHINE

Time Machine: *The Three Musketeers* . . .

"There are five of them," said Athos, half-aloud *"and we are but three; we shall be beaten again, and must die on the spot, for on my part, I declare I will never appear before the captain again as a conquered man."*

Athos, Porthos and Aramis, instantly closed in, and Jussac drew up his soldiers.

This short interval was sufficient to determine D'Artagnan on the part he was to take; it was one of those events which decide the life of a man; it was a choice between the king and the cardinal; the choice made, it must be persisted in. To fight was to disobey the law, to risk his head, to make at once an enemy of a minister more powerful than the king himself; all this the young man per-

ceived, and yet, to his praise we speak it, he did not hesitate a second. Turning towards Athos and his friends:

"Gentlemen," said he, "allow me to correct your words, if you please. You said you were but three, but it appears to me we are four."

"But you are not one of us," said Porthos.

"That's true," replied D'Artagnan. "I do not wear the uniform, but I am in spirit. My heart is that of a musketeer; I feel it, monsieur, and that impels me to go on."

"Withdraw, young man," cried Jussac, who, doubtless, by his gesture and the expression of his countenance, had guessed D'Artagnan's design. "You may retire, we allow you to do so. Save your skin; begone quickly."

D'Artagnan did not move.

"Decidedly you are a pretty fellow," said Athos, pressing the young man's hand.

"Come, come, decide one way or the other," replied Jussac.

"Well," said Porthos to Aramis, "we must do something."

"Monsieur is very generous," said Athos.

But all three reflected upon the youth of D'Artagnan, and dreaded his inexperience.

"We should only be three, one of whom is wounded, with the addition of a boy," resumed Athos, "and yet it will be not the less said we were four men."

"Yes, but to yield!" said Porthos.

"That's rather difficult," replied Athos.

D'Artagnan comprehended whence a part of this indecision arose.

"*Try me, gentlemen,*" *said he,* "*and I swear to you by my honor that I will not go hence if we are conquered.*"

"*What is your name, brave fellow?*" *said Athos.*

"*D'Artagnan, monsieur.*"

"*Well, then! Athos, Porthos, Aramis, and D'Artagnan, forward!*" *cried Athos* . . . .

Time Machine: *The Plainsman* . . .

FADE IN *on a tall, somber-faced giant, in dark coat and matching hat, polished black boots, two walnut-handled Colt .45's, worn reverse-fashion in the frontiersman's twist, jutting from his lean middle, approaching the front steps of JOHN LATTIMER'S TRADING CENTER. A burly, moustached Army Sergeant, uniform worn casually, leaning against one of the supporting wooden posts, suddenly blocks the tall giant's path, barring his way. It is 1876, a warm, sunny afternoon and James Butler Hickok has a gun duel appointment with Lattimer, who has been selling rifles to hostile Indians.*

"*You'd better take cover for a few minutes,*" *Hickok advises in the tight, thin-lipped delivery of actor Gary Cooper.*

"*You act as though you own this town.*"

"*I'm just walking through it.*"

"*And us fellows,*" *the Sergeant snarls surlily, taking a step down, further blocking Hickok's forward direction,* "*can get out of your way like we was dirt —*"

"*Suit yourself.*"

Hickok tries to step around him but the Sergeant now confronts him directly, tugging a cigar from his brutal mouth.

"Alright, Mr. Long Hair — you're too dern friendly with Injuns to suit me!" Seemingly unnoticed, two soldiers, one on either flank, position themselves advantageously for the gunfight that is sure to come. On a nearby buckboard and behind a post.

Wild Bill Hickok stares icily at the Sergeant from his position just below him.

"You shouldn't have said that, Soldier."

"Whaddya gonna do about it, you gun-totin' windbag?"

Realization shines in Hickok's cold blue eyes.

"Oh — substituting for Lattimer, eh?"

"What of it — ?"

Hickok steps back. Disappointed but determined.

"Well, I can't shoot at that uniform. If you want action, take it off!" The offer is flat and deadly calm.

"Yeah — ?" the Sergeant snarls belligerently, "an' get a slug while I'm doin' it — ?"

"Take it off!" Wild Bill Hickok commands sternly, moving further back for a clear field. "I'll give you that much time. I never draw on a man who isn't ready —" With arms fanned out, away from his gun butts, James Butler "Wild Bill" Hickok is ready.

This is all the Sergeant needs. He too steps back and begins the false gesture of pulling off his Army jacket. But his tell-tale side glances to his waiting confederates signal the beginning of hostilities.

Even as Hickok tugs his Colts from their high holsters, the ambushing soldier on his left squeezes off one deliberate round that finds its mark in the giant's arm. The impact of the bullet drives Hickok to the hard earth. Now the soldier in hiding on his right opens up. And the burly Sergeant goes for his own weapon. But once the unfair advantage is lost, Wild Bill Hickok is in full charge of the fight. Now, the famous Colts thunder and lip flame and sound. The soldier on the left topples from the buckboard, the one on the right is dead before he hits the street. The Sergeant is blasted at close range from Hickok's prone position before him and below him. When his own gun explodes, the slug tears harmlessly into the wooden planks of the steps leading up to the Trading Center. Veteran Charactor Actor Harry Woods dies nicely.

Hickok struggles erect, agony etched in his lean, handsome face. All around him shouts go up, voices cry out and the air is filled with the galloping rhythm of a horse coming as fast as it can. A familiar voice bellows: "BILL! BILL!"

It is William Frederick "Buffalo Bill" Cody arriving just in time, summoned by Calamity Jane....

Time Machine: *High Noon...*

"Why does it have to be you, Will?"
"I have to go back — that's the whole thing...."
Marshall Will Kane turns the buckboard

around and heads back to Hadleyville to restore Law and Order for one more day while the three gunnies down at the railway depot wait for the noon train which will bring crazed Frank Miller back to town for his final showdown with the lawman who sent him to prison....

I had to go back, too.

I did. It was the bottom line of Everything.

Will Kane. They should have spelled his last name *Cain*. For what else had he tried to be but *His Brother's Keeper*, just like in the Bible? That was Gary Cooper, too, in all the great movies. And wasn't it what I had tried to be down through all the bullet-riddled, crazy-cases years? Something was wrong someplace, though. Things hadn't worked out. My life hadn't worked out. Murphy's Law had descended upon me with a vengeance. The Walter Woody caper had finally put all my machinery out of commission. I was convinced I had died and instead of going to Heaven or Hell, I wound up in some cosmic cuckoo-land where I was never going to be granted Eternal Sleep or peace of any kind. Earth, Outer Space, Manhattan or Nowhere — I didn't belong anyplace. There seemed to be no final landing place for a carbon-unit like me.

"That's not logical, Captain." Like Mister Spock always said to Captain James Tiberius Kirk on the bridge of the USS Enterprise. Pointed-Ears said it all. Even if "Bones" McCoy never agreed.

"Open the Pod Bay doors, Hal." David

Bowman, astronaut, talking to Hal, the Super-Computer. The Machine that will finally ruin us all.

Halina had opened all hers for me in my stainless steel fantasy-nightmare. And what did that mean but more mindlessness?

I had become Dr. Morbius's *'mindless primitive'* on that forbidden planet of Altair. The *Id Monster* had claimed me completely. Taken me over, devoured and digested me. Ed Noon *kaput.*

But I had to go back again.

Like I should have done in the first place.

To the Beginning. *Genesis.* Where it all started.

On that Jumbo jet, designated a 747, eating up the white clouds and blue skies some forty thousand feet above the limitless prairies and deserts and mountain ranges of these continental United States. Where there was no Dr. Charles Covington, no Halina, no Helen Hamlet and certainly not a Zavoda or Harachai or Detective Sergeant Poe O'Connor whose mother read Edgar Allan to him as a child. No Gary Cooper, either. Not the ectoplasmic one, anyway.

Wyoming, wasn't it? . . . Spread out down below like a rug . . . .

When I was rapping with the little man in the white suit, one Maximiliano Sacco, and Miss Woodburn was still off somewhere in the powder room and Malvina the curvaceous stewardess was shaking her lovely rump, winning the wide central aisle . . . .

I wanted to live again . . . *live!* . . . Just like George Bailey's second chance in *It's A*

Wonderful Life . . . Zu-Zu's petals forever . . . .
I didn't want any more Clarences.
Only angels had wings.
I loved Jean Arthur but I loved life, too.
Even more.

17.

SPECIAL EFFECTS, MAN

Rollback: Sometime in September, 1987 . . .

. . . Sacco had been stabbed . . . .

"Señor —" Staccato, spurting gasps parted his lips. *". . . They stop at nothing, you see?"*

From all sides, voices swirled, loud and low, boxing me in. The screaming woman had turned off, too. I heard a child whimpering and someone else sobbing.

". . . Woody . . . Woody . . . liquidate Roland . . . for him . . . for me . . . Señor Noon?" He *was dying in my arms . . . .*

"Sure, Max. Stop talking, will you?"

The knife had dammed up the flow of blood from the wound but the internal damage of cold steel tearing through a man's vital parts, that was something only a medico and x-rays could solve. I cradled the little man in my arms, snarling out loud for that doctor or someone, anyone, with medical expertise. Who never did show up. A jet full of S.O.B.'s but luck of the draw. Not a single M.D. this flight. And Time couldn't wait for Maximiliano Sacco ... *as it had not waited for me* ....

There was a great and thunderous *whooshing* roar and the whole universe pitched at right angles ....

... A blasting, booming explosion of violent upheaval and destruction. Skyrocketing at us from somewhere close to the nose of the ship. The thunder and the disintegration volumed at us from that direction .... *The nose? Hadn't it been the tail?*

... Sacco died in my arms, the knife jutting from his small back like the flagmarker on the eighteenth hole ....

... And the jumbo jet was yawing, veering, tilting ....

... *Bomb on board* ....

... bodies flew ... cartwheeling ... scattering .... The 747 dropped down in a death dive ... straight down ... the impossible angle ... power-diving for green Wyoming below ....

Women and children blurted out their terror.

Men screeched and bellowed. *Bedlam owned us all* ....

All of our separate worlds were wrapped up in one tiny pin-point of Time. One step from Eternity.

This was my Moment.

Where the Madness had begun.

What could I do to stop it?

Halt it, check it —
Make it all make sense.

Un-warp the Time Warp. Take it out of Warp Drive.

Settle the unsettlement. Solve the Unsolveable.

Un-confuse the confusion. Straighten up and fly right.

From my agonized position, jammed against the plexiglass window on the left side aisle with a woman and her child crammed into my arms, huddling for protection, I saw it all. Watched it like a man in a dream. The great wide green flat earth rushing up to meet my eyes. And the 747. Enormous patches and swatches of desert yawned beneath us. The jumbo plummeted. Closer, closer, closest. Suddenly, the total universe was my private picture of the Earth beneath us. The air was charged with the keening siren of angel wings flapping, hell-hounds baying . . . God laughing . . . .

I could not stop anything.

The 747 struck Wyoming at a speed of better than five hundred miles an hour. With all the stops out. Metal screaming.

Struck Wyoming face first, with its nose gone.

Walk away from that one, Ed Noon.

And did anyone tell you today?

Death *is* greater than leaving town . . . .

It was a place that seated about six thousand people. There had never been a movie theatre like it. They used to call it the *Showplace Of The Nation*. It deserved the title as no place ever could or would again. They don't show movies there anymore but when it opened in 1932 it was the grandest theater of them all. With or without the flashing, dazzling legs of an army of chorus girls on stage, dancing in military unison. I never went to Radio City Music Hall for the Rockettes alone, as much as I dug women. It was the movies that brought me, breathless and excited on the subway trips from the far-off Bronx and walking tours when I hung my hat in Manhattan. Those magical miles of celluloid.

My first marvelous encounter was on October 27th, 1939 when I cut school because it was my birthday and made my maiden voyage to Manhattan. *Mr. Smith Goes To Washington* was the cinema attraction that day. I walked in at ten o'clock, got lost in the great organ playing, the stage show and the movie and didn't leave until I sat through everything three times. I was hooked forever. As the years rolled by and I grew, Radio City and Ed Noon were interchangeable. There wasn't a show house like it anywhere in the world. Even when I traveled in War Two and saw the other side of the map I learned the truth of what I had known as a boy. Home had it all.

And now I was sitting in the Great Hall again. Just as I always had, where I always had. About ten rows back from the Great Stage. Only there wasn't a picture playing. There was no program at all. And no one was in the Hall but a handful of people I knew.

All sitting in the row behind me. Not talking, not indicating anything. Just sitting. The house was dark. No lights. Only the gloom of its magnificent interior. The *Cass Parmentier*, the organ player, was not at his little niche in the side wall. The place was alive with memories. And ghosts walked, unhampered, all over the vast area. I saw Gable, Tracy, Colman, Edward G. Robinson, Garfield, Boyer, March — some of them usually played the *Capitol* or the *Strand* but they all belonged here . . . even if they weren't the familiar faces sitting silently in the gloom of the row of seats behind me . . . I heard Bogart's dry laughter from somewhere up above me. Flynn, Tyrone Power and Robert Taylor joined in. Not too many ladies, for somehow, most of them were still alive. They always seemed to outlive the men. Of all the lady superstars, only Joan Crawford and Norma Shearer had taken a taxi. The rest, Dunne, Davis, Colbert, Stanwyck, Young, Arthur, Lupino — were still kicking. The insurance companies ought to look into that one.

The people in the row behind me were old friends now.

I saw Maximiliano Sacco, Dr. Charles Covington, Halina, Zavoda, Harachai and one shadowy figure that had to be Gary Cooper. The head was higher than the other ones. I did not see Mike Monks, Melissa Mercer or Detective-Sergeant Poe O'Connor. Which somehow told me something. There was no Walter Woody or Richard Roland. That told me something too. I was dealing with the purely unreal, the imaginary. Or had I gotten my images crossed?

Sacco's eyes were closed as though he were dead, Covington still wore the bloodied bandage swathing his forehead, Halina's ungodly eyes were glowing while a soft smile played about her lush lips. Zavoda and Harachai were solid blue shadows — that was the only reason I could tab them. As for the taller shadow, the outline of a ten-gallon hat was unmistakeable. That and the characteristic rakish angle. But nobody was doing any talking —

"All right," I said, out loud, my voice seeming to roll around the enormous amphitheatre. "Who's going to open up first? We haven't got all day for this, you know."

I heard a laugh. I think it came from Zavoda, the Noseless One, but I wasn't sure. Still, nobody answered me.

"Nobody?" I snapped. "Nobody at all?"

Nobody. That was their collective answer.

I was sure they had all heard me. I sounded like a Greek Chorus. But mourning never became Noon. It never had.

The Hall was now a vast tomb. An enormous funeral parlor. Me and my shadows seemed to be holding a gigantic wake.

"Where's Walter Woody?" I asked, as deliberately as I could, "and above all, where is Richard Roland, the man I am supposed to have strangled for a million dollars?"

A solitary finger suddenly poked my shoulder from behind. I did not have to turn around. It was a Cooper gesture, all the way.

For immediate confirmation, his tight-lipped, clipped drawl echoed in my ear:

"Up there, Ed. Look up there. You're looking right at them."

I looked. The view was telescopic, framed.

On the Great Stage, where two football teams could have scrimmaged, I saw two figures. Both men. For a long, unbroken moment, I stared. It was like watching the nightmare unfold, the fantasy dissolve, taking solid shape at last. The two unseen question marks, the mystery men, the twin enigmas, were here at last. And I wasn't going to let them go right away. They came as advertised.

Standing, as if at attention. A great spotlight had come on from somewhere behind and beyond us. Shining down on the pair of people — one of whom was not supposed to exist — ringing them, leaving them with no escape. Surrounding them with a halo of light that was unwavering, unblinking. I did not need any of my ghostly company, including the Great Gary, to tell me which was which. Who was who. These books could be judged by their covers.

The man on stage left wore a rumpled, soiled white suit with matching scuffed canvas sneakers. He was tall, gaunt and stooped. A shock of very white hair, leonine and unruly, topped a craggy, leathery face from which peered two eyes that looked like grapes soaked in alcohol. The [*compleat*] Millionaire-Who-Likes-To-Walk-Around-Looking-Like-A-Bum. The woods have been full of them since the very first miser king.

Standing stage right was his direct antithesis.

A flawlessly dressed young dude with a tailor's delight of a wardrobe and the looks and the figure to go with it. Wavy black hair, coal-black eyes, white teeth, bronzed skin and an altogether winning facade plus animal magnetism plus bucks.

The rich wino looked like he needed a doctor and three nurses in constant attendance. The handsome gigolo type appeared primed and ready for a Broadway production number.

"If the bum is Roland and the rich one Woody then I'll never get out of this," I muttered, half to myself but the Cooper voice murmured, "You called it, Ed." None of the others said anything. It looked like it was going to be my show.

Walter Woody and Richard Roland, front and center, looked out at me. And down. Both of their faces were curiously alike. The expressions, I mean. Sort of a watchful waiting.

"Aren't either of you going to say anything? Anything at all? I think I am owed an explanation."

Now, they turned to each other and exchanged glances, then their faces came back to me again. The rumpled wino character nodded and coughed suddenly. An opening-the-discussion-cough if I ever heard one. The rheumy eyes almost twinkled with amusement.

"Mr. Noon, you have been granted a great gift. A very special gift. One that is not handed out indiscriminately." The voice was a combination of John Huston, Jason Robards and Orson Welles. Whiskey-baritone with booming echoes. "Do you know what that gift is?"

"Some gift. You unscrewed my head, took it off, put it back again. And you do it any old time you feel like it."

"Don't be glib and flippant." Walter Woody crooked a warning finger at me. "Think, you fool."

I hung onto my nerves. And my sarcasm.

"Okay. I died. I got born again. I died again. And here I am back with all the people I didn't know existed a few months ago. Not counting the Ace, of course. He always existed for me."

"Is that all you think about, Mr. Noon? Nothing else?"

"It's your story, Mr. Woody. You tell it."

The Richard Roland figure stirred.

"You will have to explain it to him. He doesn't understand. You, the Legend. I, the Killer of the Dream. Perhaps it would be remiss if you did not tell him all there is to tell. From the very outset of his fantastic voyage."

"From the picture of the same name?" I shot at them. "Come on, for Christ's sake — I haven't got all day — I'm due back in my coffin any old second now —"

"There is no coffin, Mr. Noon," Richard Roland intoned.

"Nor is there death for you. Not just yet." Walter Woody chuckled dryly. "It will amuse you to know that you will pass the year Two Thousand. You are one of those fated to live a long, long time. Despite your notions to the contrary."

I shook my head, still conscious of the silent group just behind me. The Angel at my shoulder. The phantom Cooper.

"You're making that up. It's not possible — the plane — Sacco — the bomb — all this mental roller-coastering. I *have* to be dead — none of it makes any sense otherwise. . . ."

"It will," Walter Woody almost purred. "If you will only listen and stop thinking about yourself."

"Then talk, for God's sake. Tell me. I'm listening."

"Look at the screen, Mr. Noon. The Great Screen. There you will find it all. As you always did when you were a child. Open your eyes, Mr. Noon. Look — see — understand —"

Walter Woody and Richard Roland suddenly parted. A neat maneuver that might have meant six points on a football field. Their contrasting figures seemed to dissolve, stage left and stage right. I heard a fanfare, a blaring union of brass and drums. The enormous white screen that had always dominated Radio City abruptly filled the world. I started to rise from my seat but a firm restraining hand on my shoulder urged me back down ever so gently. It was Cooper's hand. It had to be.

I relaxed, the drum and bugle sound cascading from the white screen. The whiteness faded to black, there was one great moment of darkness. An eternity, maybe. But probably no more than a split second. The music was unfamiliar but I somehow expected the MGM lion or the Paramount or Warner Brothers logo trademarks to fill my eyes. They didn't. There were no opening credits at all. The music died out as quickly as it had begun. All at once, there was a nothingness. Only the darkness and the uncertainty, the unbearable suspense of not knowing what was coming. Hitchcock built an entire directorial career on that sure-fire suspense technique. *The Thirty-Nine Steps* all the way.

It came.

The screen came to life.

FADE IN on an interior. Fashionable, modern, pleasant.

An airplane's interior.

A deluxe modern skyliner. With two aisles and three rows of seats. There I was. And Maximiliano Sacco and Malvina sashaying down the long aisle. I saw Miss Woodburn in the background, squeezing delicately out of the jumbo jet's powder room. I saw all the faces of the S.O.B.'s that had surrounded us. Somehow very familiar now, like old friends and family — I looked at myself and did not like what I saw. The face was untypically cruel and cold. I was wearing an expression that belonged on Jack Palance in *Shane*.

Nobody was talking. I could not hear a sound track.

It was like a silent movie but traveling at normal speed.

And then the fun started. Fun and bad games.

The pandemonium, the McGuffin, the excitement.

Maximiliano Sacco was reeling toward me and the camera, the killing knife jutting from between his shoulder blades.

The mysterious bomb exploded once more. The Big Bang.

And the big screen gave me the simple answer, the final solution to all that had plagued me. Bugged me, brainwashed me.

It was right up there before me, as plain as Life.

And as murky as Death.

We, all of us on that doomed 747, had been attacked by forces from Outer Space. *The rhythm of the spheres* . . . .

Aliens, Extra-Terrestrials, Invaders, Strange Ones — Creatures From Another Planet — eerie weirdies . . . .

And not Creatures From The Black Lagoon. No way.

Force Five, boys and girls —

Who had come to conquer America.

And not with a song in their hearts.

Only power, beyond belief.

Total Power.

18.

RETURN OF THE ED EYE

In war-torn Fortress Europe, George Long had saved me from a sniper's bullet once. But not even he could stop Force Five from getting me. In the End. Force Five wasn't going to let anything and anyone put the kibosh on their plans. Thank You, Step Down, Next Contestant Please. Armageddon, Anybody?

The jumbo jet did not nose-dive, go into the straightdown death drop I remembered. It halted. Stopped dead-stop, perfectly still in midair. Each and everyone of the S.O.B.'s, the women, the men, the kids, Malvina, Miss Woodburn, Maximiliano Sacco and I, froze in the Statues Game. Everybody stood still in the posture they were in when the miracle struck. Whether caught standing, falling, sprawling, flying with arms and legs out-stretched — whatever. It was a freeze-frame all around. A Still Life that would have baffled a Rembrandt, a Van Gogh, even Dali. The picture no artist could ever have painted. Or wanted to.

I watched, mesmerized, from my ghostly seat in the darkened row in the limitless Music Hall. The wide screen up above was unrolling, unfolding with what had actually happened on Flight 717. The Greatest Story Ever Told — maybe — Madness, certainly.

The interior of the jetliner plunged into darkness. Not like a light winking out, either. There was a ghastly blue glow to the scene. The figures of the people, mine included, flattened out to no more than tall blue shadows. Like weird silhouettes framed against the special blue screen of a film maker's special effects field where you can pull off any kind of cinematic trick in the books. Like making spaceships fly and meteors and planets and asteroids come to life. The total impact is mind-boggling. It was, *now*.

It lasted no more than a minute, the blue darkness, the ghostly painted-people-upon-a-painted-ocean tableau — and then the cabin lights went on again. And the jumbo was hurtling earthward and me and all the rest were bouncing around like rag dolls in a descending 747 that had to be doing better than five hundred miles an hour. All the sounds came back, too. The screams, the wails, the shouts, the sobbing — the terrible, desperate, frantic frenziedness of the human race when it knows it is seconds from death. And Extinction. I know. I was one of them.

And I was scrambling and clawing like a terrified rabbit caught in the headlights of a car too close. There was *Finis* up there on that screen. In glorious Technicolor and stereophonic sound. Music by Max Steiner.

The jumbo jet hit Utah.

Pancaking in on a crumpled landing gear, roaring across the desert landscape, between all those gorgeous buttes and then coming to a lurching, shuddering stop, the huge tail section rising up like Moby Dick from the choppy Atlantic.

But I knew, better than anyone, that something had happened in that magical mysterious moment up there in the Wild Blue Yonder. When Something Blue, Something Incredible, had taken over the plane. And taken over us. Our bodies and our minds.

Which was why I was able to suddenly understand why I could see myself walking with a still-alive, no-knife-in-his back Maximiliano Sacco. Just me and him out for a stroll in the wide open spaces. With no 747 in sight. No crash. No other passengers. Only the gleaming ball of hot sun, the vast panorama of buttes and Western landscape. Mad Max and Crazy Eddie. What a team. Without the Fancy Songs and Snappy Patter.

"Max, Max."

"*Señor?*"

"I think I understand now, Max. I can see the whole thing now. I couldn't before — how could I? But I can, Max."

"That is good, *Señor* Noon. *Bueno.*"

"I know now why you aren't dead, the way you should be. And why we're out for a nice stroll like this when we both should be pushing up daisies."

"*Como?* — I do not know that expression, *Señor* —"

"*Flores por los muertos*, Maximiliano. It wasn't my time yet. About you I don't know — you little old android you."

"Again you confuse Sacco, *Señor* . . . ."

"Sorry. That's right. You're a replicon, not an android. Fresh off the little old Planet Bardo. And you asked me to kill Walter Woody for a million dollars. Because an outer space outfit called Force Five needs him to take over the world and you Bardons being such friendly guys don't want that, right? Which is why you came to me. But — and a big one — Force Five beat us all to it. They caught up with us both on the plane up there. Several hundred thousand light years from their own planet."

The little heavily-tanned man in the white Panama suit stood before me, shaking his head. But his eyes gave him away. You can always tell by looking at the eyes, Man or No-Man.

"The bomb, *Señor* . . . ."

"A freak. Something you didn't count on. Or Force Five. Just some guy who had nothing to do with any of this finally deciding to end it all. It should have changed everything but it didn't. And it didn't stop Force Five from doing its magic act. Its specialty."

"And that is . . . ?" The wily little man was

fencing with me, now. Acting the cautious turtle, afraid to poke its head out.

"Snatching the body and identity of everyone on that jumbo jet. That plane came down safely — something that never could be according to the laws of gravity and aerodynamics — unless Force Five wanted it that way. The blue light and the blue shadows tipped me off. Which means Force Five has planted over two hundred of its own kind on this Planet Earth. Over two hundred enemy aliens walking and talking like the people they have replaced. The enemy within — the old Commie and Nazi trick. They'll be here for years until Force Five is ready to strike in force. The full follow-up to their Invasion."

Maximiliano Sacco placed a forefinger to his forehead and wiped away a trickling bead of perspiration. The daylight sun was a scorcher. But the air was soundless, timeless. A dead zone.

"If what you say is true, *Señor* Noon, then how did we manage to escape? Why are we not with the survivors of that plane crash this very moment?

My teeth were clenched in a grin.

"Simple. You aren't flesh and blood, are you? You can't be cloned and you have some tricks of your own. And me — Sacco, I'll tell you something. When a man has been a detective all his life, when his mind is a permanently working shop of clues, puzzles, ideas, solutions — and wonder — that man is not so easy to take over. I don't know why but Force Five couldn't snatch my body.

Mike Monks must have been right — I'm a hard man to replace."

"Then —" The little man smiled. "Why is it we are here — talking to each other, like two *amigos*? Why do we dally?"

"Because, my little brown buddy, I've been lost and trying to find myself. Wandering around for months, half-in and half-out of the world I knew so well. Having dreams and nightmares and delusions. I'm having one now. A master dream to make this all add up for myself. *Comprendez?* I'll be leaving you soon enough and maybe we'll never meet again but I know what this is all about now. Like I told you. You're the last link. And I'm sitting out there in Radio City, a few rows back, with some of my other fancies and delusions and soon I'll really know where I am. But right now, I'm with you, you fugitive from Bardo, and I'm asking you, where do *you* go from here?"

Maximiliano Sacco stared up at me. He still looked like *El Exigente*.

The expression in his dark eyes was now not quite normal. Imagine a machine looking at you or a pay telephone taking your measure. He was no longer flesh and blood.

"They will find us and take us both to the hospital and I will disappear," he said.

"Yes," I answered.

"You shall be declared mentally unbalanced and be placed under the care of a *médico* named Covington."

"Dr. Charles Covington," I agreed.

"You will seemingly recover and return to

your business practice. *El investigatore privato.*"

"You got it."

"And all this will remain unexplained, a secret. Known to no one but yourself and myself and the members of Force Five."

"I hear you talking, Max."

"I am sad, *Señor*. For myself and you. And the planet Earth. The Walter Woody hoax will continue. Deceiving all. Force Five will ultimately gain its objective. But, *Señor* —"

"Yes, Max?"

"It was a great run, was it not, *amigo*? For moments, you held the secret of the universe, the magic of the cosmos in your fingers. When you do go back, you will now remember nothing. This I pledge to you. It is the way of these mind flights. Thought control and brain reversal is yet an imperfect thing. Even for such superior forces as ourselves of Bardo."

I frowned. "Come off it, Max. I'll forget nothing. I remember Mama and everything else that ever happened to me since I first saw Coney Island and Christmas trees and city lights —"

"No, *Señor*." His tone had the finality of forged steel. "You will not. Not even a unique man such as yourself can hold in your head all that is there now. Your rebellion is done."

"You're trying to tell me something, Max —"

He showed me something, instead. His tanned right hand came up, holding a weapon. Something that looked like a hand-gun but I knew wasn't. It was short, stubby, conical and completely black. Shaped like an ocarina but I somehow knew it wouldn't make music.

"*Adios, Señor.* I have enjoyed your company."

"Max, don't — " I took a step toward him. He did not back off. "Not just yet. Please. I'm not finished asking questions —"

"But you are, *Señor.*"

And I was.

The ocarina-weapon flashed like a red light. Something hummed. Droned. A shaft, a ray of something, shot from its muzzle. Hitting me directly in the chest. There was a cataclysmic burst of radiance, like a nova exploding. And Maximiliano Sacco, Utah, the buttes, the blazing ball of sun and the desert vanished. Hiroshima must have gone up like that. Life and death all in one crashing, thundering second. I faded to black in an instant. Not a tall blue shadow, no. I was the Incredible Shrinking Man, wisping down to nothing. Toward Zero, into the Void. Infinity. Limitless Outer Space again.

And I was back in Radio City Music Hall in my seat once more.

The big screen had gone totally dark. The last picture show.

I twisted in my darkened seat and looked behind me.

Endless row-upon-row of emptiness mocked me.

There was nobody sitting there.

Dr. Charles Covington, Halina, Zavoda,

Harachai, Walter Woody, Richard Roland, had deserted me. Ditto Gary Cooper. I was the only customer in a six-thousand-seat movie house.

I didn't feel anything. It was as if there was no blood, no flesh, no sensations to me. My mind was a total blank. There was no pain, no confusion, no elation, no depression. No anything.

I don't know how long I sat there.

When the house lights went up and the hall gleamed with full exposure, I did not move. I was sitting like a kid, waiting for the picture he had liked so much to come on again.

The muffled footsteps coming down the wide center aisle made me turn around at last. They were footsteps I had somehow expected.

I saw Captain Michael Monks of Homicide and Melissa Mercer of the Noon Detective Agency hurrying toward me. Monks' grim face was a study in granite and Melissa's lovely mask was etched in dry-eyed grief. I smiled at them, waving a hand in greeting.

They drew to a slow stop beside me. Frozen in motion.

Monks looked down at me. I could see he was holding Melissa's hand tightly, as if he would never let go.

"Hello, Ed," Monks said in a low voice. "I knew we would find you here."

19.

OH, GARY,
WHERE ART THOU?

There was a sun again.

A bright burning fiery ball in the bluest of
blue skies. The grass lawn stretching out
before me was greener than any golf course.
From my wheelchair seat on the stone patio
behind the building that housed the lunch-
room, I could see a long way off. I didn't
know the name of the mountains that lay in
the background, sloping gently East and
West. It didn't matter anyway. I wasn't going anyplace anymore. Sitting and looking
was about all I could manage these days.

Two squirrels worrying each other over a
random piece of popcorn suddenly parted
before me and raced to the tall mimosa tree
that stood maybe fifty yards away. I laughed.
The squirrels had looked like the Marx
Brothers doing a routine, Chico and Harpo.

Groucho wouldn't have bothered.

I was all by my lonesome. Everybody had split after lunch, going off to do whatever they had to do that afternoon. Lunch had been no great shakes. Typical bland hospital food. Rubber chicken, flat toast, limp salad, watery coffee and fruit salad that tasted like it had been in the can too long. I didn't care anymore. Food meant nothing to me. I had too much to think about.

A shadow fell across my chair. Someone had gotten between me and the sunlight. I squinted, shading my eyes with my right hand. The white suit was unmistakable. White uniform, really. Something that hasn't changed since Kildare was a pup. Make that Louis Pasteur out of Paul Muni. This was my Florence Nightingale.

"Oh," I said. "It's you again."

"Someone to see you, Ed."

He stood to one side and the sun burned me crisp. He was tall, thin and gangling. Lantern jaw, sensitive mouth and eyes plus a black, shining cowlick. He was a ringer for the younger Jimmy Stewart. I folded my arms and checked out the mimosa tree. The squirrels had vanished. So had my peace of mind.

"I don't want to see them. And I don't want to see anybody. And yes, you do look like James Stewart, Lester."

"Sure I do. Everybody says so. But how about that company? It's going to be a long afternoon and you could use a visit. Some talk with your old friends."

I sighed. "Sure I could. But I don't think I know them. Anyway I can't remember them.

And that black beauty is always crying. And that guy with the face of a bartender — look, I know they mean well, but what good is it? I don't know who they are. I never will."

That made Lester take a beat. Gave him something to think about.

"They're trying to help you get your recall back. Can't you see that? Talking may unlock your memory — it happens sometimes. Come on, Ed. They're very nice people."

"Sure they are."

"Besides, looking at a doll like that ought to be good for what ails you. And that Monks is a pretty sweet guy for a cop."

"Sure he is."

"What do you say, Ed?"

I spread my hands. There was no use arguing with Lester.

"Okay, Lester. You win. Trot them on out. But I swear to God I'm not going to do this again. Not ever. Everytime they come, I try and try — and the look in her eyes stays with me long after they leave. Like I let her down or something. And him — Christ, I can't remember who my father was but he'll do very nicely, thank you."

Lester's voice rose on a happy note.

"That's the ticket, Ed. And thanks. I promised them I'd really talk you into this. They know how you feel."

"I'll bet — get going, Lester."

He practically ran off to get them. I checked the mountain range. Somehow I had never seen anything that looked so eternal, so peaceful. As if it had been there, just like that, lying blue and brown in the sunlight since Adam and Eve. A Genesis slide.

They came along in what seemed like seconds later.

The tall, broad-shouldered, barrel-chested cop. He was a Captain or something, he had said. And the black woman. She was something all right. Trim, classy, moving in a graceful glide, even with three-inch spikes on her shoes. They were both smiling as they came up. Gallows smiles. They couldn't fool me.

I was hopeless and knew it. They knew it too.

I waved to them. The man shook hands with me. He had a wrestler's grip. The black woman simply put her hand on my shoulder and squeezed, gently. Her eyes told me a lot more.

They both began to talk, at the same time. I nodded, half-hearing them, murmuring something or other. They were nice folks, very nice people, and I wished I could help them by being who they wanted me to be. I had tried. Real hard. But I never came up with anything concrete. And it always ended the same way. They would talk, try to urge me into something, and then I'd get edgy and unhappy and I'd start wishing they would be gone. It was getting like that now. The way it always did. I never should have given in to Lester. But he was such a nice kid and I always liked anyone who looked like Jimmy Stewart. *Well, I guess this is just*

*another lost cause, Mr. Paine . . . all you people
don't know about lost causes . . . .*

Beside, the gang would be showing up any
minute now and I didn't want any strangers
hanging around. Not even nice people like
the cop and the black woman seemed to be.

Sure enough, even while they were still
talking, I could see the gang coming up over
the hill. I saw the plumed hats first and then
Athos, Porthos, Aramis and D'Artagnan
came into view, arms ringed, talking,
laughing. The way they always did. Then the
Geste Brothers, Beau, Digby and John.
Classy guys, all. Cyrano de Bergerac and
Scaramouche crossed the horizon, followed
by Don Quixote, that Man of La Mancha.
Gray though he was, he was great fun, and
what a talker. Right behind him was Robin
Hood, who always looked like Errol Flynn.
And then, the voices of the cop and the black
woman really faded into nothingness. Into
silence. I couldn't hear them anymore.

A very tall, elegantly lanky frontiersman
loomed into view, stalking toward where I
was sitting on the stone patio. The giant in
buckskins, the twin walnut-stained handles
of the two Peacemakers, gleaming in the
afternoon sunlight, marking him for me for
all time in all my memories. My soul quieted
down.

I relaxed. I was happy. At peace, again.

The gang came swarming down from the
hillside, the lone cowboy in the van, giving
me the familiar, old-time hand signal.

The air was alive with the sound of vitality and excitement. And friendship. Nothing else really mattered.

I settled back in the wheelchair, waiting for them all.

Gary Cooper was smiling at me.

The slow, full smile.

The one that told me that everything was all right again. No matter what the cop and the black beauty were talking about. Worrying about — trying to do for me.

Coop was back.

That was all that mattered.

THE OUTER LIMITS OF
TWILIGHT ZONE

Scaramouche, *nee* Andre Moreau, who had been born with a gift of laughter and a sense that the world was mad, held up his hand for silence. The laughing, joking crowd of heroes who had been larger than life and more than ten feet tall, all broke off in mid-conversation and looked at the young poet askance. The devil-may-care Moreau was ever the one to think of something brilliant to do on a long summer afternoon.

"I have composed a poem, gentlemen. A tribute as it were, to our mutual friend sitting there in the wheelchair."

"Let's have it then," Athos spoke with his familiar authority, motioning Porthos, Aramis and the ebulliently youthful D'Artagnan to be still. "M. Noon is more deserving than most men of my acquaintance. When an individual has survived countless duels and trials he is fit to be called our comrade-in-arms."

Robin Hood smiled, a twinkle in his roguish eye. "Would that I had had him at my side in Sherwood to battle Prince John, Sir Guy of Gisbourne and the foolish Sheriff of Nottingham."

The Geste Brothers were all in accord with that, too.

Michael nodded gravely. "I would have dubbed him Sir Edward as a child and when we defended the walls of Fort Zinderneuf, and who can say — he might have saved my life from the wily Tuareg and I could have delivered the cursed *Blue Water* to Aunt Pat in person instead of John doing the errand boy for me."

Digby Geste chuckled. "Then you would have missed your Viking's Funeral, Beau. No dog at your feet."

John Geste said soberly: "I for one wished he had. And you too, Dig. No lark watching you get shot in the back of the head by that beastly Arab sniper."

Don Quixote de La Mancha stirred, his wise old eyes reflective.

"It is true enough. *Señor* Noon is an honoured companion. My beloved Sancho Panza would have worshipped him as he did myself."

The enormous nose of Cyrano de Bergerac sniffed the afternoon air. He made a flourishing gesture with his arm as though his sword were unsheathed.

"Burn me but it is I who should have put

together several stanzas, nay, a sonnet to our cherished Eduard — *'and when I end the refrain . . . put out my hand in homage!'* "

Andre Moreau flung back his head and laughed.

"He shall never hear my tribute if all of you continue to talk. May I commence — subject to your pleasure?"

There was a rousing chorus of laughter and agreeing sounds of urging. The man in the wheelchair could not speak. He was too overcome with the joy of knowing and being with this august group of genuine heroes. Men whose like the world would never see again. They were *non-pareils*, all of them. Each and every one.

Andre Moreau began to speak, orating in his fine voice.

"Not just for any guns he fired true
Nor damsels in distress he did accrue
As much as for the reason rich or poor
He always did the client cure.
Not just because his bleeding heart
For Mankind ever took the part
As much as for the ideal, fine and high
He always made his banners fly.
In love and battle, he ever fought off ruin
This man the angels named Ed Noon . . . ."

A reverent hush fell over the assemblage when Scaramouche had finished. For a long moment, no one spoke.

The silence was broken only by the gentle sobbing of the man in the wheelchair.

Everyone doffed their hats and placed them at their hearts. Gary Cooper's eyes were moist. The group stood still.

Homage to a comrade-in-arms.

A man who had always been one of them.

*   *   *   *   *

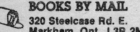

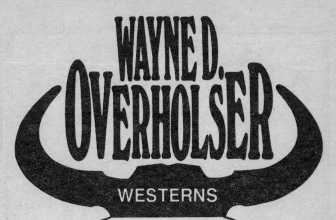

WAYNE D. OVERHOLSER

WESTERNS

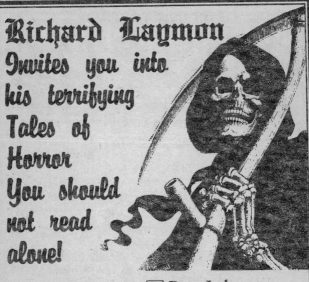

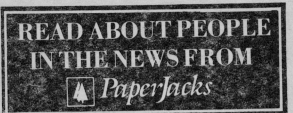

FREE!!
BOOKS BY MAIL
CATALOGUE

BOOKS BY MAIL will share with you our current bestselling books as well as hard to find specialty titles in areas that will match your interests. You will be updated on what's new in books at no cost to you. Just fill in the coupon below and discover the convenience of having books delivered to your home.

PLEASE ADD $1.00 TO COVER THE COST OF POSTAGE & HANDLING.

BOOKS BY MAIL

320 Steelcase Road E.,
Markham, Ontario L3R 2M1

IN THE U.S. -
210 5th Ave., 7th Floor
New York, N.Y., 10010

Please send Books By Mail catalogue to:

Name _____
(please print)

Address _____

City _____

Prov./State _____ P.C./Zip _____

(BBM1)